HOTT TAKE

A STEAMY RUSH CREEK ROMANTIC COMEDY

HOTT SPRINGS ETERNAL
BOOK 2

SERENA BELL

1

SHANE

In all the years I've been a leading man, I've never actually felt like I was *in* a movie...but there's a first time for everything.

Also, I'm clearly not the star of the show here. That role goes to Weggers, our grandfather's attorney—a short, balding guy with the general aura of a kids' movie villain. He takes his job extremely seriously. He stands behind me, offering me a sheet of thick, creamy paper with as much flourish as the server at a Michelin-starred restaurant.

I wish it were a menu of anything other than my doom.

"Please read it aloud," Weggers instructs.

I glance around the conference room at my family members. They all meet my gaze, except my sister, Hanna, who is frowning at the table like it canceled her favorite streaming service. My brothers mostly look amused and slightly sympathetic—plus relieved that they're not in the hot seat. Quinn has been here before and gives me an eyebrows up cocky grin, like, *How's it feel now, asshole?*

Not so hot, I'll be the first to admit.

"*Shane*," Weggers prompts.

I squirm in my uncomfortable cheap-office-furniture seat but obey. "'Famous is as famous does, Shane Hott,'" I read, wincing.

Not that I actually thought my grandfather would go easy on me. But I guess I'd hoped he'd singled out our brother Quinn for the worst treatment. Quinn recently had to read a similar letter out loud. It instructed him to spend two months sitting at a spa reception desk, which is a fate worse than death for a guy whose people skills include grunting and frowning.

I guess I was just hoping that all the rest of our letters would say…I don't know, maybe, *Just kidding! You don't actually have to jump through any hoops to save Hanna's land!*

Nope.

Weggers signals an impatient *Continue*, and I read: "'Hott Springs Eternal has done a good job at putting itself on the local map, but to attain the kind of success Hanna and I envisioned—'"

My sister howls with rage.

"This is *not my idea!*" she cries. "I told him to leave you guys alone! I said he was going to piss you off! I said he had to get over the fact that you were your own people and needed to do your own things!"

My brother Preston—wearing a suit that's straight out of central casting for "finance guy"—puts a hand on her shoulder. "It's okay, Han. Nobody thinks this is your doing. You're not devious enough for this kind of bullshit."

Hanna crosses her arms and sulks. I'm not sure if it's because my grandfather threw her under the bus or because she's pissed we don't think she's devious.

"Please keep the interruptions to a minimum," Weggers intones.

If you wrote this guy into a movie, no one would believe it. They'd shut the TV off in the middle of episode two and write a scathing Screenflix review about how unfair it is that everyone hates on lawyers.

I know plenty of good lawyers and plenty of bad ones, but this guy carves out a whole new territory for himself. He would be the comic relief—except there's nothing funny about my grandfather's will.

The will leaves the ranch land we grew up on to my brothers, Hanna, and me.

Sort of.

What it actually says is that we have to hold our grandfather's ranch land in Rush Creek without selling it for two years, during which time we must obey any instructions our grandfather has issued. These instructions come on our grandfather's time line and in a form specified by him. Namely, letters on expensive paper delivered in Weggers's conference room, around a heavy, over-polished table, surrounded by books no one has read since Weggers graduated from law school in the Jurassic period.

If, and only if, we follow all those instructions, we keep the land and it won't pass to Blue Iron Mining and be stripped of its mercury and other heavy metals.

If, and only if, we follow each and every last whim of my dickwad grandfather, my sister will get to keep her birthright and the amazing wedding business she runs on the land.

"Carry on, Shane," Weggers says, waving his hand like I'm the hired help.

I bury the impulse to off him with one of his oversized law books and read:

To attain the kind of success Hanna and I envisioned, Hott Springs Eternal will need a wedding that garners national, or even international, attention.

A celebrity wedding.

My stomach drops like the Tower of Terror.

You, Shane Hott, celebrity, are perfectly positioned in your well-connected LA life to recruit a celebrity couple to be married at Hott Springs Eternal. You have six months to make a celebrity wedding happen.

"No," I blurt out.

My eyes snap to Quinn's. I don't know what I think I'll find there, but if I was looking for sympathy, I'm SOL.

He smirks and says, "Accept your fate, dude."

And shit, it serves me right. I've always given Quinn a way harder time than I should. He's just so…teasable. I may or may not have made his life hell recently, as he was trying to deny his feelings for Sonya.

Lesson learned: never alienate the guy who might be on your side when the tables are turned.

"I can't plan a wedding." I cross my arms. "I have a movie to shoot. Next week."

"I have excellent news for you!" Weggers says—which is clearly a lie because he wouldn't smile that evil dark-lord smile if the news were actually good for us. "You don't have to plan it. Hanna will plan it."

"I—what?" Hanna's eyes get huge.

"You"—Weggers points to me—"just have to supply the willing celebrities."

"That doesn't sound so bad," my aunt Meryl pipes up,

finally tearing her eyes off her knitting.

If it were anyone other than Aunt Meryl, I'd glare at her, but she's so well meaning I can't do it.

"Not bad at all," Weggers says. "Your grandfather isn't trying to make life difficult for anyone."

There's a loud sound—the combined scoffs of a whole room full of six-foot-plus, broad-shouldered, hyper-competent Hott brothers—and one pissed-off sister.

"What, exactly, is he trying to do, then?" my brother Rhys asks.

"He's merely making sure you're all worthy of this gift," Weggers tells us.

The sound this time is synchronized gagging.

"Wait," Hanna says. "What's this bit about me having to plan it?"

Weggers holds up a finger. "There are some additional stipulations. As you'll see when you read onward."

Pretty sure you can hear our coordinated eye-rolling, too.

I find my place and continue reading. "'The wedding must be planned by the lead wedding planner at HSE.'"

Hanna groans. "So, me."

"Looks like it."

"That was my idea!" Weggers crows. "I wanted to make sure Hott Springs Eternal got the business. Otherwise Shane could just get them married in Hollywood or Vegas."

"Thank you," Hanna tells him darkly.

"You're most welcome." Weggers gives a nod of his head that might be a bow.

No sense of irony, this one. I read: "'The couple must both be celebrities and must be in—' *What?!*"

"Must be in love," he supplies, as if I've asked a real question instead of just choking on my saliva.

"*Be in love?*" I repeat.

"Yes. Be. In. Love."

"How am I supposed to guarantee *that*?" I squint at him. "And how are you supposed to *know* that? You can't read their minds."

"I can read their *behaviors*," Weggers says. "Your grandfather has entrusted me with judging for myself whether you meet the terms of the will and his other instructions—"

"I should have contested!" my brother Rhys cries.

"You *definitely* should have contested," I growl at him. "Remind me again why you didn't contest!"

Rhys looks at Quinn. Quinn looks back at Rhys.

"It wasn't entirely a rational decision," Rhys says. "It just..." He shrugs. "And then it kind of..." He doesn't seem to be able to finish the sentence.

"Didn't happen," Quinn says, unhelpfully.

We all stare at both of them because neither of them is a guy who's ever deliberately evasive or vague. Rhys is a family attorney—read: shark of a divorce lawyer—and Quinn is a brilliant scientist.

"They didn't want to fuck things up for me," Hanna says.

We all turn to look at her. She rolls her eyes at us.

"Just admit it, guys," she says. "You did it for me. And now it's too late to contest."

We all squirm. No one speaks. But we do hang our heads, remembering how her husband, Easton, pulled us aside and ripped us a collective new one about being shitty brothers.

"We haven't exactly done the best job ever of being there for you, Han," Rhys says.

It's an understatement. My brothers and I got the hell out of Dodge—meaning Rush Creek—as soon as we could. And I'm pretty sure all of us have questions about whether we did the right thing. Or maybe that's just me.

"No," she agrees—which is Hanna for you. Honest sometimes to the point of bluntness and refreshing as hell. "But this is too much to ask of anyone."

She looks tired. And guilty. Hanna is one of those people who has boundless energy and never bothers with unnecessary emotion, so seeing her like that makes me feel...

Like a shitty brother.

"It's not that bad," I say. "I mean, all I have to do is recruit a couple. There are a million people in Hollywood falling in love every day."

"Are there?" Rhys asks, scowling. He's our resident cynic —not that any of us has a glowing opinion of marriage and family life, but you can imagine that our divorce lawyer brother has the worst view of both.

"There are," I say, which makes Hanna perk up, and that's really all I need to see.

Because if anyone's been a shitty brother, it's me. I left and never came back, not even for Hanna's wedding. And for what? The least admirable reason of all—fame and fortune.

I plant my hands on the table and stand. "I've got this, guys. How hard can it be to come up with one celebrity couple who are actually, really, and truly in love with each other?"

2

<hr>

FIVE MONTHS LATER—IVY

My ex-boyfriend, Anthony Fessa, is sitting on the front stoop of my house in Rush Creek.

And the worst part is when I get out of my car, start up my front path, and see him, my heart gives a teeny, tiny leap of joy.

You'd think that particular organ would have been too broken by Anthony's treatment of it to even try to leap...but apparently old habits die hard.

Even though my heart and I are supposed to hate him, he looks good sitting there, surrounded by the early May flowers blooming in my garden and the recently painted white picket fence. Broad-shouldered, strong-jawed, built like a movie actor—which is to say someone who spends a huge amount of personal effort on eating right and working out so there won't be an ounce of fat anywhere it's not supposed to be. The effect is—well, more or less the same as it was the first time I laid eyes on Anthony. He's, objectively, gorgeous.

Plus once upon a time, I thought I might come home to Anthony and a white picket fence...

But this is not a fairy tale.

"Ivy," he says in that professionally trained, butter-soft, deep, rich voice. "I've missed you."

Luckily my heart is *not* in charge of this operation. My brain—captain of the ship—kicks into gear and says, *We don't negotiate with assholes.* And I say, "No, you haven't, Anthony. What do you want from me?"

Because if I learned anything from my thirteen months with Anthony, it's that he doesn't do anything without a reason, and that reason always serves him. If he flew all the way up to central Oregon from LA, it's to get something he wants.

"Don't be like that, Ivy. We had something special. It just ran its course."

"It ran its course because you got what you wanted from me and moved on to exploit someone else for your next gains," I point out. I don't add *leaving me and my life in shambles*—but I could have. I was a mess after Anthony ended things.

But that was then, this is now, and I have everything I want: my picket fence, the community theater I run, someone in my life I can totally trust (even if that person is my sister).

I don't need or want Anthony in my life, and I won't let him unsettle me.

Captain Brain, take it from here.

"Good talk," I say. "Can you just move over a bit so I can get into my house?"

He rises to his feet, towering over me at six feet plus.

"Okay, look, you're right," he says. "I owe you an apology. I should have stood up for you when the producers were making the decision about writing your character out of the show."

"Damn straight you should have."

"I'm sorry," he says.

I experience a small melting event, more on the ice cube than the ice shelf scale, but I can feel my shoulders sinking and some of the tension goes out of my body. "Thanks."

"Can I come in so we can talk?"

I can feel myself caving. Not because I still have feelings for him (I really, really don't), but because it was a long day at the theater with the kids and I'm wiped.

"We can talk right here."

He frowns. "At least sit down."

"Are you going to tell me you're pregnant and it's mine?" I joke.

"Just sit."

I do. He sits down on the stoop a little distance from me.

"Hear me out," he says.

"You're scaring me."

"There's nothing to be scared of. This would be a good thing for both of us."

Why do I doubt that?

"If you've been following my career, you'll know it's stalled out a bit..."

I have been following his career, but I'll be damned if I'm going to admit that to him. Sometimes in my lower moments, I Google him to see if he's scored the lead in some Hollywood blockbuster yet. The answer's no. After

Bridge—the show we were both on—ended, he got a part in another Screenflix show, but they only made two seasons. Then he was in a streaming movie, but as far as I know, it faded rapidly into obscurity.

I wasn't exactly *happy* to see that he hadn't broken out...

But I was...

Happy.

Okay, I'll admit it. I was glad the universe hadn't rewarded him for his shitty, user behavior.

I shrug. "Haven't followed."

"I fired my manager and hired a new one with more publicity background. And she thinks I need to..." He pauses.

I'm sitting here, trying to figure out what any of this has to do with me. I left LA four years ago and never looked back. When I was there, I wasn't exactly the queen of managing my public image brilliantly. I had a manager and an assistant who took care of my social media, and I did okay, but I'm not any kind of genius. People don't come to me for publicity advice.

"She thinks I need to get married."

Oookay, those are *not* the words I was expecting to come out of his mouth.

"And she thinks I should marry you."

3

IVY

"He said *what!?*"

My sister Nia's mouth hangs open.

"He said he wanted us to get married. He wants to stage a yearlong, very public engagement with lots of involved planning that we can get lots of *Bridge* fans sucked into so he can build his platform and raise his value to producers. He wants to do a proposal that plays off Oriana's big stupid speech about wanting someone to come along and save her from loneliness and fill her up with babies—"

"No," Nia says flatly. "He is not serious."

"Pretty sure he's deadly serious. Obviously I said no."

"*Obviously,*" she says. "Holy shit, Ivy, what a narcissist."

"I know."

She gives me a big hug. "Hey. I'm sorry that happened to you. That's so uncool of him."

I wave a hand. "Whatever. It's over. I told him no, he begged and pleaded and said I was the only one in a position to really help him make a splash—"

"And you said, 'You should have thought of that before you let them write me out of the show.'"

"And I said, 'I'm really fucking tired, Anthony. You should leave so I can go to sleep.' And he did."

She hugs me again and strokes my hair. "I'm sorry, kiddo."

"You know what was the worst?" I say.

"What?"

"I just wanted to be able to say, 'I can't marry you, you narcissistic prick, because I'm happily married with two kids and a very floppy-eared rescue mutt.'"

"You'll find someone," she says.

"Preferably someone who has never heard Oriana's 'the end of the universe is lonely' speech or jerked off to a scene of her getting boned in the engine compartment."

I'm referring to the fact that I do periodically get avid fan emails or messages from horny guys. Some are marriage proposals, offering to help me with my "all alone in a big universe" problems. Most of them, though, have spent too much time replaying the other famous Oriana *Bridge* scene and want me to help them out in person with their fantasies...

"Good luck," she says. "Maybe you could settle for one who has a firm grasp on the difference between reality and fiction?"

I laugh. "Please. God, if I'd known when I knuckled under and filmed either of those scenes how they'd come back to haunt me... Okay, you know what? Let's never speak of Anthony Fessa or his ego-stroking idea again. Distract me with some fun news."

She wrinkles her nose, pondering. "Got it. Did you know Shane Hott is in town?"

"Who?" I say.

"Shane Hott. The fae lord in the *Crown of Spires* trilogy."

My face must display utter blankness because Nia rolls her eyes. "Seriously, Ivy? You haven't watched the *Crown of Spires* movies?"

I give her a *Really?* look.

"I know you don't watch a lot of stuff, but no *Crown of Spires*? At least you must have read the series."

I shake my head.

"World in peril, hot alpha fae lord, and here's the connection—hottest scene in all of television—spire sex."

"What is *spire* sex?"

"She's lashed to a spire, and he— You really need to see it for yourself."

I shrug. "Sounds very dangerous."

"In the best possible way," Nia moans. "You have to watch this scene."

I roll my eyes.

"Your loss." She shakes her head. "I know you shun everything LA, but I'd think by now local gossip would have dished up Shane Hott and the fact that he's actually *here*."

"I avoid local gossip, too." It's true. I stay off social media, I stay away from big gatherings, and if people start whispering, I run the other way instead of sidling closer. I had enough of all those things during my LA years—back when I lived and acted as Eva Scott—to last the rest of my life. "But Hott sounds familiar—oh! Hott as in Quinn Hott?

"I know who *he* is. His company made that miracle drug Dad took."

"Quinn's his brother," Nia says. "Shane's the movie-star brother. There are five of them. Each hotter than the last. Hotter!" she cries, delighted, and I roll my eyes again.

Quinn's pretty yummy—but *definitely* taken, if I remember correctly from my last sighting of him with the manager of Hott Spot, the local spa and salon, on his arm. And I don't do fellow actors—understatement of the millennium—so that knocks out Shane as an option. Not that I'm shopping. Seeing Anthony again reminded me of why celibacy is a great idea.

Never trust a guy so good looking he makes you stupid. Say it with me, friends.

The door of the old church bangs open, and the first few high schoolers straggle in. Nia and I run a community theater in the town where we both live, Rush Creek. We offer a bunch of after-school programs for kids, mostly middle and high school aged. Today is improv day, which is my favorite.

We greet the kids, give them time to glom snacks and unwind a little, then corral them onto the stage. The church —former church, actually—is an old congregational one, New England–influenced white clapboard on the outside, with a steeple and everything. Inside it's darker than I'd choose, some of the wood paneling peeling, desperately in need of repairs and upgrades. But we don't own it and the owner has been on a round-the-world trip, so there's a lot of deferred maintenance.

That reminds me, actually—our lease is almost up, and I need to email the owner about signing a new one.

Our company doesn't have enough money yet to build a theater of our own, so we're just grateful to have this church. Several years ago, Rush Creek, a former rodeo town that was looking for its new purpose, gave birth to an outpouring of brand new hot springs. Overnight, the town spawned spas and wedding venues—and pretty much all the retail and performance spaces got snatched up by people who wanted to profit off the new opportunities. So the fact that we have this amazing theater-friendly building...most days, it feels like a miracle.

"Okay, peeps," I call to the kids. "Let's do some warm-ups. Let's start with Ball Toss."

I toss the imaginary ball across the circle to Garrett, a junior with a sandy-blond bob, and they catch it and wing it to the next person. It goes around like that until I tell the kids it's not a ball, it's a hot potato, then a basket of kittens, then a baby, then a ball of slime. The game ends when Justin yeets the ball of slime straight at my face and I "fail" to put my hands up until it's too late, then have to sluice the imaginary slime out of my eyes and flick it at the members of my class. Everyone's laughing and relaxed by the time we're done.

It warms my heart. Some of these kids barely smiled and never talked to each other when they first started coming here. They've come out of their shells in a big way.

I'm about to launch them into one of my new favorite improv games, Curfew, when I hear the creak and slam of the church's big front door and look up to see an unexpected face. It's Jillian Megler, the building's owner. I knew Jill and her husband, Jason, were planning to return from this trip sometime this spring, but I definitely wasn't expecting her yet. Or here.

I glance to Nia. *You good to take over?* I mouth.

"Yup," she says, and I trot down the stairs and toward the back of the church, where Jillian is leaning against the wall.

"Hey," I say. "Welcome home." I open my arms, and we hug.

"I was hoping I'd find you here," she says as she releases me. Her eyes rake over my face, and there's a tight, nervy tone to her voice. Alarm bells go off in my stomach. "I, uh, need to talk to you about something."

Her eyes find the high school students on the stage— hard to tell from here exactly what they're doing, but they're in whole-body improv mode, and laughter rings out from their peers in the audience.

"Jill..." I say, like somehow I can keep her from telling me whatever this piece of news is that she has to share, but she blurts it anyway, in a big rush:

"I can't renew your lease, Ivy. We're turning the church into a wedding venue. Starting in three weeks."

4

———————

SHANE

Hanna hands me her phone, a grim look on her face. We're sitting in her office at Hott Springs Eternal.

"What?" I say.

"Just—watch." Her lips flatten.

I recognize the background in the reel. It's Christopher's, one of my favorite restaurants in LA. January Stark and Tobias Bauer are seated together at a candlelit table, holding hands. Smiling.

"This is good, right?" I ask Hanna, my eyes flicking to her face for reassurance and finding none.

January and Tobias are my celebrity couple, the ones who'll get married in a month and help me fulfill the terms of the will. Finding them was *not* easy. I spent five days driving all over LA like a guy trying to work the traveling salesperson problem, interviewing celebrity couples to make sure they were in love. Correction: to make sure they had the acting chops to convince Weggers they were in love.

Just when I thought I might be the brother who destroyed Hanna's business and turned the Hott land over to environmental ruin, I found them. January and Tobias, young Hollywood up-and-comers who'd bonded over a shared affection for Shonda Rhimes, sushi, and rage rooms. They knew Hollywood could eat up couples and spit them out, but *their love was different.*

Which was good enough for me.

Since then, Tobuary/Janbias have planned their wedding under the sharp eye of Weggers...and passed muster.

Then this morning, Hanna texted me, *Meet me in my office at 9. I'll explain when you get here.*

As I watch on Hanna's phone screen, something catches January's eye. She looks up and past her fiancé. The *something* enters the frame; it's Lilla Thornton, Hollywood's current It girl, dressed to kill in a lady-in-red dress that plunges so low in the front that I wonder if she has it on backward.

Lilla says something to January—out of range of the phone's mic—and then January's on her feet, reaching for Lilla's throat. A moment later, the table flips, the women wrestle on the floor, and the tablecloth bursts into flame. The last thing you can see and hear on the reel is January shouting at Tobias: "It's over! You hear me?! It's fucking *over.*"

"No," I say, staring at the wreckage, unable to look away as the reel starts over again with happy Tobuary.

Hanna frowns. "You seem to think that just by saying that word, you can keep bad shit from happening."

"It works pretty well for me a lot of the time," I admit,

still unable to look away from the disaster that is my celebrity wedding.

"I got a call from January a few minutes ago," Hanna says. "She canceled the wedding."

"Nooooooo," I howl.

She gives me a look. "Shane. It's over. It's done."

"No," I say, more firmly. "We are not giving up."

Hanna folds her arms and closes her eyes briefly. "You have a month to produce a wedding, Shane, or we're straight-up fucked."

"We could ask Weggers for an extension? Or you know, like, an exemption. Or a rules change?"

The look of scorn she gives me could shame a nun. "No way Weggers will violate the letter of the law."

"He might," I say, but both of us know he won't.

Hanna and I have gotten close over the last few months, bonding over this farce of a wedding, baby Eloise's developmental milestones, and—following their low-key, friends-and-family exchange of marriage vows recently—bets on how long it will take Quinn and Sonya to make little Hotts. I have my sister back, and I won't lose her again—let alone be the guy who destroys her business or ruins our land. "What if I call them and beg them to get back together? Does the will say I can't bribe the celebrity couple?"

"It says they have to be in love," Hanna reminds me.

I wave a hand. "It says Weggers has to believe they're in love. So I just need them to make up...convincingly and publicly."

I'm already reaching for my phone, dialing up January, who is the more level-headed of the couple. That's not saying much, but I'll take any edge I can get.

"Jan," I say when she answers.

"It's Maria," the voice on the other end of the phone says. Maria is Jan's personal assistant, best friend, and maid of honor. I personally think it's ill-advised to put so many eggs in one basket, living in the den of snakes that is Hollywood, but it seems to work for them.

"Maria," I say, relieved. "It's Shane. I saw the video."

"That *fucker*," she growls.

"Please tell me it's just a blip."

"It's not just a blip. It's the last straw in a very, very large hay bale."

"No," I say, and Hanna groans on the other side of the desk.

"Can you put January on?" I ask.

"January is not taking phone calls right now," Maria says.

I rub my free hand over my face. "Please, Maria," I beg. "If you help me make this wedding happen, I will ensure that you and all your friends have gainful employment in film for the rest of eternity."

She snorts. "That's a really generous offer, Shane, but it doesn't do me any good."

"Why not?"

"Because you're not going to change January's mind."

"How can you be so sure?" I ask.

"Because Lilla is pregnant with Tobias's baby, and they're getting married this afternoon. At Lilla's parents' estate."

5

SHANE

When I hang up the phone with Maria, I turn my attention to Hanna across the desk. Her head is in her hands.

"How much of that did you hear?" I ask.

"I couldn't hear any of her end," she says without lifting her face from her palms. "But you said, 'How can you be so sure?' and then your face went this really awful vanilla-pudding color, so the answer couldn't have been anything good."

I relay the news about Lilla's pregnancy and impending nuptials. Hanna just shakes her head, still buried in her hands.

My chest feels like someone installed a concrete block in it. If there's one thing I've learned as I've gotten to know my sister again over these last few months, it's that Hanna loves her job. She and my grandfather built this empire on the former Hott ranchland, and she's its undisputed queen. There's a lodge and a big wedding barn, the Hott Spot spa and salon, staff cottages, and campgrounds. There are weddings here almost every weekend all summer, well into the fall and spring, and during the holiday season. She has a staff of over a hundred now and loads of partnerships and relationships she's built one blunt, no-nonsense interaction at a time.

I can't fail her.

"I'm going to find a new couple," I say.

"How the hell are you going to do that?"

Still, she raises her face from her hands, hope filling her blue-green eyes.

"I don't know," I admit. "But I'm going to do it."

"Hanna," a voice says from the doorway. It's Julia, Hott Springs's office receptionist and all around keeper-of-order, a tall dark-skinned woman whose voice still holds the flavor of Jamaica, where she grew up. "Eva Scott is here to see you."

"Eva *Scott*?" Hanna says. "Like *the* Eva Scott—of *Bridge*?"

"That Eva Scott," Julia confirms.

"She wants to talk to *me*?" Hanna asks.

"Is she a celebrity?" I demand.

"Oh, she's definitely a celebrity," Julia says. "But don't make a big deal about it. She's been hiding out in Rush Creek since she left TV, and rumor has it she's *very* private."

"Does she *need to get married*?" I ask, ignoring the warning in Julia's voice.

"Not that I know of," she says. "She wants to ask about using the new small barn for a couple of months. Something about a theater group."

"Ask if she needs to get married," I hiss at Hanna.

"Out," my sister says to me, pointing at the door. "Get

out. I am not going to start asking random people if they need to get married."

"It's your business I'm trying to save here!" I remind her. "Go!"

I do, but not far. I linger in the hallway, tucking myself into the alcove of a nearby locked door.

It wouldn't help anyway if Eva Scott were planning to get married—not if she were marrying a civilian. She would need to marry a celebrity. And what are the chances that a "very private" actress wants to marry a celebrity?

Pretty close to nil.

Julia leaves and comes back with—

Tall. Slender and curvy. Golden-haired, like the color of sunshine. Her mouth set in a perpetual, wry almost-smile. A glow like she's lit up from within—but also a magnetic girl-next-door freshness.

Holy shit.

It's her. My golden girl.

It's the woman I crossed paths with months ago when Quinn was working at Hott Spot. Sonya told me her name was Ivy Scofield—but Eva Scott must be her stage name.

Now I understand why Ivy—or Eva—struck me as too beautiful to be a mere mortal. She's not. She's an actress.

The girl-next-door thing is probably a well-honed act.

An act that is *definitely* working on me because I'm rarely, if ever, attracted to actresses. But this one—

I groan internally.

The first time I saw Ivy/Eva, I wanted her.

But I didn't know how much till I saw her talking to Quinn and felt an overwhelming urge to muscle my brother out of the way—and, preferably, out of Earth's orbit.

I find myself suddenly hoping that Ivy/Eva is *not* contemplating getting married. I don't know if my inner caveman can hack it.

I strain my ears to hear the conversation coming from Hanna's office.

Ivy's slightly husky voice: "I'd just need it for a few months. Until we can find another venue. Even a few weeks would help us. Just—there's nothing, and someone mentioned you'd had construction delays and hadn't been able to start scheduling weddings for this spring, and I was hoping—"

Hanna's no-nonsense reply: "I wish I could help, but we just finished construction and have to start booking weddings ASAP."

"I can pay you whatever you'd be able to get for putting weddings in there."

There's a murmur, Hanna's voice dropping out of audibility, and I know she's said the price out loud.

"Oh," Ivy says. "No. I don't think we can...no. We can't afford that. I'm—I'm sorry I took up your time."

"I'm sorry, too," Hanna says.

I can tell she means it, but I'm still caught on the crushed hope in Ivy's voice. For whatever reason, using our small barn for her theater group matters *a lot* to her.

And for reasons I don't understand at all, I want to fix this. Need to fix this. I need to make this okay for her.

An engine turns over in my brain.

Ivy needs a thing.

I need a thing.

Ivy is a celebrity.

I'm a celebrity.

One celebrity plus one celebrity equals two celebrities.

Ivy steps out of Hanna's office looking as miserable as my sister looked ten minutes ago.

"Excuse me," I say.

She startles and looks up at me. I wait—then realize that what I'm waiting for is recognition. I'm waiting for Ivy to get the *oh, that's Shane Fucking Hott!* look in her eyes—but she doesn't.

I usually *hate* that look of recognition because it comes before a whole lot of other bullshit. Inappropriate questions, needy requests, sexual propositions.

Except this time, for a change, I'm disappointed.

"I'm Shane Hott. Hanna's brother," I say. *Also Mavryx Extyllior, Lord of the Fae. Actor. Very rich. Very successful. Very good in bed.*

I don't say any of that, but it's a close thing.

Apparently I have gotten used to having my reputation precede me because it galls me that she won't know all those things about me.

I'll have to actually earn her friendship, trust, and—eventually—adoration.

So. Much. Fucking. Work.

And yet oddly...I'm looking forward to it.

6

———

IVY

After Nia told me that Shane Hott is an actor, I watched the first *Crown of Spires* movies, *Lord of Every Sky*. It was full of scenes where he was shirtless, badass, and bossy. He's basically the villain of the first movie—although I get the sense that he's going to be redeemed later from the way the camera lingers on his...assets.

Even as I watched, I questioned my life choices. I wasn't at all sure watching the movie was a good idea because in a town as small as Rush Creek, Shane and I were bound to cross paths.

After I watched him in *Lord of Every Sky*, I wanted to build a small monument to his torso and worship it...with my tongue.

And now, encountering him in the hallway outside of Hanna's office, my knees feel less solid than I would ideally like.

Never trust a guy so good looking he makes you stupid.

So I do what any self-respecting woman would do in that situation.

I pretend I have no idea who he is.

I can tell he's waiting for me to recognize him, giving me a beat to say, *Holy crap, Shane Hott!*

After he got on *Bridge* and turned into a household name, Anthony used to do the same thing.

Seeing echoes of Anthony in this guy makes me even less inclined to give him what he wants. Another Hollywood fuckboy hopped up on fan worship. It's the last thing my life needs.

"Nice to meet you. I'm Ivy Scofield," I say, cool and low key, like I'm introducing myself to the manager at the bank.

Surprise flickers behind his eyes, but he hides it, extending his hand. I take it. It's big, warm, and dry and, unfortunately for my equilibrium, attached to a toned, muscular forearm below a rolled shirt sleeve. The shirt itself is a soft-looking blue gray that clings in all the right places to his movie star–worthy shoulders, pecs, and abs. He has long-lashed dark brown eyes paired with a blade of a nose, square jaw, and lush mouth. Against my will, I admit that he's gorgeous.

I thought I had permanently rid myself of men who were too good looking to be believed, but apparently not.

"I think we can help each other out," he says. Actually, he whispers it. "You, um, mind walking with me?" He gestures toward the exit.

"Should I be worried that you're a serial killer?"

The corner of his mouth turns up. "I'm not a serial killer. I'm an actor."

"Even worse."

He laughs, which is terrible because it makes him even better looking, all eye crinkles and white teeth and genuine amusement. Then he stops—because I wasn't joking and he seems to intuit that.

"Even so," he says, more seriously. "Please. Just...let me walk you out and tell you what I'm thinking."

I give him a shrug-nod, and we walk out of Hott Springs together to the parking lot. Now I know who owns the Aston Martin Vanquish I parked next to. I know nothing about cars...but Anthony coveted that car: fast, expensive, and—his words—a dream to drive.

As we draw even with his car, Shane says, "I know you need our barn."

I flick him a quick, confused glance as hope buys real estate in my chest. It sounds like he's implying that it still might be possible. I will do anything to save our theater—not just for me, but for the kids. I know Nia feels the same way.

"I can get the barn for you."

"Hanna said—"

"Hanna wasn't looking at the whole picture," he tells me. "I am."

I raise an eyebrow.

"You need the barn, and I need you to marry me."

His too-pretty-for-real-life face is deadly serious now. My mouth falls open.

What. The. Fuck.

So many marriage proposals, so little time.

"Did you just say...?"

"Yes. I need you to marry me. In a month. On June third, to be exact."

I rearrange my face to be less *holy shit* and say, "That's—oddly specific." I feel like someone pulled the rug—no, actually, the whole floor—out from under me.

He nods. "There's a lot of wedding preparation already in place for that day. It just needs a bride and a groom. A celebrity bride and groom."

"Is this about how you need some buzz? You need a better platform? You want producers to see how much value you'll have for their next project?"

Something like amusement crosses his face. "Uh, no?"

"Then—what?"

"I'm going to tell you, but you're not going to believe it."

"Try me." I cross my arms.

His eyes flick briefly to my chest, then—so quickly I'm not sure it really happened—back to my face. "My grandfather's will says I have to plan and execute a celebrity wedding within six months—five of which have already passed—or Hanna loses Hott Springs Eternal and this land."

I vaguely remember buzz about Shane's brother Quinn...something about Quinn having to work at the reception desk of Hott Spot—also because of the family's land. "Your grandfather had some interesting ideas about what goes in a will," I say.

"That's one way to put it." He rakes an aggravated hand through his styled-to-be-bed-headed hair. I wonder if it's as soft as it looks or slightly plastic with expensive product. I wonder so hard that I have to actually consciously not reach out my hand and touch it.

I'm losing the thread—and this situation definitely

demands all my attention. "So you're saying…if I marry you, you'll let me have the barn for the theater."

"Yes."

His expression's dead serious now—a slight furrow in his forehead, thick well-formed eyebrows, lush lips, the perfect dusting of stubble on that rugged jaw—all his attention on me and the ridiculous question he's just put to me. It's pretty clear to me that if Satan tried to cut a deal with me, this is the exact form he'd take. Also that agreeing to Shane's proposition would be nothing more or less than bargaining with the devil.

What isn't clear is why I'm so tempted to say yes.

I need to pause and think about why this is a terrible idea:

He said the wedding will take place in a month—that's a whole month I'd have to be in the orbit of a man who, in addition to being a Hollywood fuckboy in his own right, reminds me of my first and worst Hollywood fuckboy.

He described the wedding in question as a celebrity wedding, which makes it pretty clear that we'd be the center of a publicity shitstorm—something I want in my life again about as much as I want a case of shingles.

At the end of that month, I'd be *married to*—and then, presumably, *divorced from*—Shane Hott, a state that would persist for the rest of my life. There would be no getting away from reminders that I'd sold my soul, however briefly, to the devil.

It seems like the answer's obvious. There has to be another way to solve my theater problem.

"No, thank you."

Shane stares at me. I get the distinct feeling that people,

especially women, don't say no to him very often. It gives me a surprising thrill.

"What are you going to do about your theater?" he asks.

"I'll figure something out. Worst case, we can rent the high school auditorium to get ourselves through the summer, and I'm *sure* something will pan out by then."

"Just to be clear," he says. "The wedding would be a sham. The marriage, too. An acting job."

"Yeah," I say. "I got that."

"You wouldn't have to do anything you weren't comfortable with."

"You mean besides marrying you?"

The corner of his mouth turns up. "Yeah. That."

"It's just a lot more complicated than my life needs to be right now," I tell him. "I moved to Rush Creek to get away from Hollywood. Away from publicity and paparazzi. Away from publicity stunts like fake marriages. Away from all that bullshit. I wanted a simple life—a job I loved and a house with a garden and people in my life that I knew I could trust."

"And did you find it?" he asks.

I'm not sure why I'm so surprised by the question. Maybe because it seems more thoughtful and less self-centered than I was expecting from a guy who up till this point struck me as just an Anthony Fessa clone. "I did."

"Who are the people you know you can trust?" he asks.

"My sister."

Wrinkles form between his eyebrows, and for a second I'm sure he's going to say that one sister isn't *people*—a thought I've had a few times—but he doesn't. He just watches me in a way that makes me feel like he can see through me.

He takes a business card out of his pocket. Hands it to me. I half expect it to be pretentious and gold leafed, but it's just a white card with black writing—his name and contact info. About as understated as they come.

"If you change your mind," he says, "that's how to reach me."

"Thanks," I say, pocketing the business card. "That's not gonna happen, but thanks."

As I walk around his car toward mine, I find myself slowing down.

I realize I'm waiting for him to call me back, to try to convince me. But he's not Anthony with his begging and pleading. And apparently he's also not his character from *Crown of Spires*. He's not going to use mind control or tie me up or play edgy games with my consent. He's just going to accept my *no*.

Huh.

That's not *disappointment* I feel, is it? Because that would be...

So, so ridiculous.

7

IVY

A few days later, Nia and her girlfriend, Akemi, come over for dinner.

I answer the door to find my sister in a pair of jeans and a crocheted top, brown hair twisted into a messy bun, and Akemi wearing a cobalt-blue sheath dress, her near-black straight hair long and loose over her bare shoulders.

Nia and Akemi have been dating for seven months. They met at a jewelry-making workshop where they discovered that they both love sea glass. Now they have a joint Etsy shop called She Sells Sea Glass, a puppy they dog-share, and plans to move in together when Akemi's lease is up.

I love Akemi. She's the ballast to my sister's cotton-candy joy. Quiet, sturdy, no-nonsense.

I hug them both tight and usher them in.

"There's a lasagna and some garlic bread in the oven, and I'm making a salad," I say. They follow me into the kitchen, where Nia and Akemi wash their hands and I offer them aprons. Akemi chooses a patchwork quilted one my mom made, and Nia hands me my favorite: *Size Matters. Ask Pluto.* She dons her own favorite, which features a range of hot pink mountains across the chest, emblazoned with *It's always Wilder in the woods.* It was a free gift as part of a wilderness foraging-and-cooking workshop that I took a couple of summers ago.

The three of us buckle down to chopping veggies for the salad.

"Okay if Nia and I talk shop for a minute?" I ask Akemi.

She waves a hand. "Go for it."

"I talked to the school district today," I tell my sister. "About using the high school this summer."

She frowns, reading the outcome on my face. "They said no, huh?"

"Yeah. Five Rivers Community College rented the space."

"Oh, right," she says. "The fire."

The college's auditorium building burned down recently—another setback in our attempt to find a new home.

"And FRCC won't sublease any time in the high school auditorium. Too many moving parts."

"Shit," Nia says.

"FRCC did say that once they've rebuilt, they'd be happy to rent their auditorium to us, but that's four to six months out."

Nia winces.

"I'm about ready to—" I laugh. "Okay, get a load of this. I didn't tell you this before because it's so ludicrous, but Hott Springs Eternal didn't exactly flat out say no."

"They *didn't*?" Nia's expression turns hopeful.

"Hanna did, but then Shane approached me and—"

"In person?!"

"Yeah, I guess he'd overheard the conversation and—"

"What did you think of him?!" she cries.

"He's very..." I abandon all attempts to play it cool. "He's incredibly hot," I admit. "I would hit that, absolutely, no reservations. I mean, except for the fact that—at least if you believe Google and the entertainment sites—he's a player and probably an asshole."

"I have heard that," Nia admits.

"Here's the truly off-the-wall thing. Brace yourself, because lightning doesn't strike twice, but: he tried to convince me to *marry* him in exchange for use of the barn at Hott Springs."

"Whoa," Akemi says, her head suddenly popping up from her intent concentration on red peppers. "I was so *not* expecting that plot twist."

"Right?"

Nia is staring at me. "Shane Hott proposed marriage to you?"

"I mean, I think that's overstating the case. It wasn't a proposal. It was a proposition. If it had been an actual proposal, I probably would have thrown something in his face."

"Fair," my sister says. "So he made you this proposition and you turned him down?"

"Understandably," Akemi says. "She's not going to marry some guy she barely knows so she can use his *barn*."

"That sounds so dirty," Nia says. "I don't even know what the double meaning would be, but there's that whole thing when your fly's down and people say, 'Shut the barn door before the horse gets out'—"

Akemi puts a hand up. "Oh God, *stop.*"

Nia smirks. She loves riling Akemi. "And barns are just —I mean, 'roll in the hay' and stud stallions and all that. Barns are very earthy-sexy."

"Can we maybe get back to Shane's proposition here?" I plead.

My sister returns her attention to me. "Why the hell would he want you to marry him? Oh, crud—I didn't mean that the way it sounded."

Akemi snorts.

"He's trying to save his family's land and his sister's business." I explain the situation to them—what's at stake with the will and Hanna's livelihood.

Nia whistles when I'm done. "Wow. That's some serious family mud."

"Right?"

"So if you help him with the will, he'll let you use the barn?"

I nod.

"Huh," she says. "For free?"

"Yeah," I say.

"Stop right there," Akemi says.

"What?" Nia demands.

"I can see the wheels turning. You're not going to sell your sister on the marriage market to get a temporary piece of real estate."

You can see why I like Akemi.

"Thanks, Akemi," I say. "And yeah, no way I'm accepting Shane's proposa—proposition. It would be a hot mess.

Getting fake married, dealing with loads of publicity and paparazzi, and spending way too much time with a guy whose claim to fame is that there's only one woman he's ever been photographed with twice. We'll find another place to house the theater."

From outside, a trumpet blares.

"What the hell?" I go to the window, pull back the curtain, and am almost blinded by the glare. "Oh, *crap*."

"What is it?" Nia says.

Outside, just beyond the fence that contains my English-cottage garden, a small band has assembled, illuminated by spotlights.

They're playing "All You Need Is Love."

My neighbors are streaming out of their houses.

I step out onto the front stoop. Anthony Fessa is clutching a microphone and wearing a tux. Off to the side, cameras capture his every move.

The band fades away.

"Eva!" Anthony cries into the mic.

"Oh, no, no, no, no," I say.

Nia and Akemi are right behind me.

"Make him stop."

"I don't think that's in my power," my sister says, gazing out over Anthony's grand gesture with a look of awe.

"Eva, I never stopped caring about you," he tells me, eyes right on mine.

"Anthony, don't do this," I say. "Just pack up, turn around, and head home."

"I didn't offer you what I know you want most in the universe—"

"I'm not Oriana!" I call.

But my words are drowned out in the next bit of Anthony's speech. "Please, Eva. I know you're lonely here in this little corner of the universe. Let me marry you, carry you off, and fill you up with babies."

"He *didn't*," Nia says.

"He did," Akemi tells her. "He most definitely did."

It's gotten very quiet. The band members sit with their instruments on their knees, watching me attentively. It's so quiet I can hear the sound of spring frogs, the music coming from an open window up the street, Nia's snicker behind me.

"I'm disowning you," I hiss to her.

The neighbors are waiting, mouths open, breath baited. Or at least I assume they're all holding their breath. My next-door neighbor has her hand over her mouth, her eyes wide.

I walk down the steps toward Anthony. He walks toward me. I can see the gleam of victory in his eyes. He caught this all on video, and a thousand bucks says his next move is to upload it to TikTok and Instagram and get every last one of our fans all-in on this ship.

If I reject him, he'll turn it into a social media event of its own and recruit every fan in our fandom to try to change my mind.

And obviously—*obviously*—I can't accept him.

My mind flails wildly, looking for an out.

And then out of the corner of my eye, I see Nia, waving her hands. Trying to get my attention.

"Tell him, Eva!" she calls. "Tell him you're..."

She doesn't finish the sentence, just raises her eyebrows

so high I hope it doesn't give her a migraine. I think she's trying to leave me an out.

But instead I grasp the lifeline she's just thrown me.

"Anthony," I say as gently as I can. For the fans' benefit. They would want me to let him down gently. "I can't marry you."

I turn back to look at Nia. She gives me a short, tight nod of approval.

I return my attention to Anthony.

"I'm already engaged."

8

___

SHANE

"Yeah," I say into the phone. "Thanks. Well, let me know if you hear from anyone who's thinking about getting married. Or getting engaged. Or pretending to get married. Or who wants to stage a really great fake publicity wedding. Or..." I've run out of possibilities. "Please."

"I will," says the two thousandth person I've made this speech to, before we hang up.

I set my phone down and indulge in a brief, quiet moment of despair, sitting on the hotel bed.

No one wants to get married.

I Googled it. Marriage is on the decline, down something like sixty percent in the last fifty years—even though you really wouldn't know it from spending time in Rush Creek, where marriage is booming business. Oregon just needs to get rid of all waiting periods for marriage licenses, and Rush Creek would be the new Vegas.

Horrifying thought.

And yet even though Rush Creek is full of people

getting married or who are just married or here to celebrate other people who are getting married...

I cannot find two celebrities.

After I asked Ivy to marry me—

Okay, I admit it. That was the worst wedding proposal ever, actually. My face gets hot thinking about it. I should have at *least* gotten down on one knee. I just wasn't thinking straight.

I don't even *know* Ivy, but I know that she deserves better than that.

After I asked her to marry me and she turned me down, I spent a couple of days thinking that maybe I'd found at least part of the solution to my problem. I don't need two celebrities who want to get married. I just need one celebrity who wants to marry me.

Except it turns out that's not that easy to accomplish, either. Because contrary to how most people think about Hollywood, there isn't just a pool of people desperately waiting to marry for public relations purposes. And if there are, they aren't as easy to find as you'd think.

My hotel phone rings.

I've been staying at the Depot Hotel, Rush Creek's premium Western-style inn, when I've been in town over the past year. It's not up to my usual standards, but it's better than camping out in Hanna and Easton's place and dealing with Eloise's iffy sleepy schedule and the large amount of moony-eyes my sister and her husband make at each other. I could stay at Quinn and Sonya's temporary place, but it's tiny, and there are even more moony eyes (and sex noises they think are subtle) over there. They're supposed to buy a house together sometime soon, but I think they secretly like the fact that they still occupy the staff cabin where they lived together when they were strangers.

"Mr. Hott," the woman at the hotel's reception desk says brightly into my ear. "There's someone down here to see you."

"Oh, hi, Alice," I say. "Hanna? Or Quinn?" Those are the two people who show up here. "Or—shit, it's not media, is it?"

"None of the above," she says. "It's—"

She stops.

"Do you prefer...?" The woman's voice is fainter, as if she's asking a question to someone else.

A woman's voice answers in the background. Then Alice says, "It's Ivy Scofield, Mr. Hott."

My heart rate doubles. "I'll be right down."

I hang up and rise from the bed, trying to pretend I don't feel tied in knots. That my whole body isn't tight with anticipation. My mouth isn't dry, my cock on twitchy high alert. *Need me? Standing by.*

None of that.

I take the elevator down and step out into the lobby, where the bar is set along one wall. The Depot Hotel is like the sound stage for a Western movie—log beams and columns, a wagon-wheel chandelier, wood paneling, lots of well-worn leather furniture—the kind where once you sit down, you'll never get up.

Ivy stands at the end of the bar, waiting for me. There's a quiet stillness to her, a watchfulness. Her eyes are on me as I approach, and I like it, being the object of her attention.

Until I get close and see that her lush mouth has lost its wryness. It's set, hard. She's upset.

"Hey," I say. "Hey. You okay?"

"I'll marry you."

Great. So the expression on her face, the *this sucks* one, goes along with the thought of marrying me.

You don't care, I remind myself. *Or you shouldn't care anyway. All that matters is making this wedding happen so you can save Hott Springs Eternal—and she just said yes.*

I square my shoulders. "Excellent. What changed your mind?"

As soon as the words are out of my mouth, I regret them —the last thing I want is to make her second-guess her decision.

She hesitates, then says, "I can't find anywhere to house the theater for the next four to six months. Summer's a big time for us—we've got camps and performances almost every week the whole summer...and I can't disappoint these kids."

So it's that. The kids.

I mean, of course it is. What did I think? That she'd pondered it overnight and decided that the world's shittiest proposal from one of Hollywood's most infamous playboys was an offer she couldn't refuse?

Hardly.

She twists her hands together. "I tried the high school auditorium, but they rented themselves out for the whole summer to Five Rivers Community College, because FRCC's auditorium building burned down—so those are obviously both out. I tried to sublease some high school auditorium time from FRCC, and they just flat out turned me down. Too many scheduling issues still pending. I said, What if I come back in a couple weeks? And they said, Don't hold your breath."

She pours that out in a rush, and I want to tell her to slow down, that it's going to be okay. I suddenly want to say she can have the barn for free, for as long as she wants—she doesn't have to marry a guy who doesn't have anything to give her.

But I can't tell her that.

I need this. More to the point, Hanna absolutely, positively needs this—and I will not let my sister down again.

"If I do this..." Ivy trails off. "You said I wouldn't have to do anything I don't want to do."

"Some affectionate contact in public. Holding hands, arms around each other. The occasional hug. Kissing only if we absolutely have to—which might happen because of the publicity piece."

She touches a finger to her lower lip, and my eyes are drawn there, the lushness of her mouth, the sight of her fingertip against the pink of her flesh. Need knots at the base of my spine, and my cock gets heavy.

Quit it, Hott. This is a fraught situation. Keep it simple.

"No sex, obviously. We live apart till the marriage, then together but different bedrooms. We divorce once everything is set with the will and the land and Weggers has backed off. I take all the blame for being the asshole—I realized I couldn't do commitment after all, I was my dick self—"

Her face creases. "That doesn't seem exactly fair..."

I shrug. "It's not like we'd be making it any worse for

me. My reputation precedes me. And this way you get all the fan sympathy."

She thinks about that. "Okay. I guess that's better than the alternative. Although sometimes fan love is worse than fan hate."

I laugh because it's true: I've seen fans do some pretty scary things in the name of adoration.

I watched the first couple of episodes of Ivy's show after we met at Hott Springs Eternal. It's a great show—well written, phenomenally well acted. I get why it was a cult hit and why people are nuts about Oriana, Ivy's sexy engineer character. The glow that Ivy gives off—it comes through on the screen. So does the girl-next-door charm.

What I don't get is why she would have walked away from it all. The show, television, fame.

But it's none of my business. I don't need to understand her to make this work.

"Okay, here's the shitty part," I say. "You have to pretend to be in love with me. Like, really. Like this is a movie we're making." I explain about the exact terms of the letter, how we have to convince Weggers we're in love.

"I'm a good actress," she says.

"I know. I watched a couple episodes of *Bridge*."

Her eyes flick to my face, startled.

"It's good. You're good. Really good."

She waves off the compliment. "Thanks. And I can do that—pretend to be in love with you."

"That means not just for Weggers but for the whole world. Family, friends, fans...the more people who will corroborate our story and stand up for us, the harder it'll be for Weggers to make a case that this isn't real. And the whole thing will be on a need-to-know basis. We don't tell anyone the truth unless we absolutely have to, and then we swear them to secrecy. We can't risk that they might out us and it might get back to Weggers."

She chews her lower lip. "I, uh...can't actually lie to my sister. Or her girlfriend. I already told them about the pro—proposition. So if I come back and tell them I'm marrying you, they'll know why."

"Can they keep a secret?"

"Absolutely."

I nod. "Okay. It's also not realistic to think I can keep it from my family, since they know what's at stake. If I show up with a fiancée, it'll be obvious what's going on. But they're all just as invested in the outcome as I am, so they'll go along with it. At least in front of Weggers, and that's all we need. We need to make it so he can't find any proof that we aren't what we say we are, even if he knows in his heart of hearts that we aren't."

"Understood."

"In return for all that, Hott Springs Eternal will give you dibs on use of the barn for—how long?"

"Six months. Then we can use the community college's auditorium."

I talked to Hanna about this after my first conversation with Ivy. We discussed whether we could postpone starting up weddings in the new barn—and still survive, from a cash-flow perspective. It's a squeeze, but it's definitely doable. And of course, the bottom line is if we *don't* make this wedding happen, we won't have a business to save.

I nod. "Six months. I can't extend it any longer than that, but we can give you that."

For the first time since we started this conversation, Ivy looks relieved. She exhales, a long rush of air that makes my own shoulders drop. "Thank you," she says. "This means so much to me. And it's going to mean even more to the kids. A lot of them have a tough time in school, are bullied, or just need an outlet for their creativity. And they need peers who feel the same way, who *get* them." She stops. "It's been lifesaving for a few of them."

The passion in her voice is unmistakable.

"I'd believe it," I say. "I remember when I discovered acting. It changed everything for me. I wasn't like some of the kids you're talking about—not bullied, not anything like that. I had my family—or at least my brothers and Hanna." *Until I left and threw in my lot with my dad.* "But acting...I felt like I'd just figured out the meaning of life."

"I know," she says, and our eyes meet. "When it's in your blood, it's in your blood, I guess. Anyway." She blushes and looks away. "I guess what I'm saying is that I'm really grateful I don't have to let these kids down. So thank you."

I feel a stab of intense guilt. It's not like I gave the gift outright, from the goodness of my heart. There's a remarkably large string attached. More like handcuffs, actually.

"Don't thank me yet," I tell her. "You'll probably be cursing me by the time we're done."

9

Shane delivers his warning, then rakes a hand through his hair.

"You, uh, have a minute to figure out our story?" he asks.

"Sure."

I figure the quicker we get our story up on social media, the less likely Anthony is to decide there's any upside to releasing his video. After last night's incident, I checked my social media a few times today, and it doesn't look like he's posted anything. Nor have any of my neighbors, which feels like a minor miracle, but I'll take it.

The idea of letting Anthony use me (again) to boost his career makes me sick to my stomach.

I'm hopeful that Nia's quick thinking and the hit to Anthony's pride will keep him from making me his pawn this time.

Anthony shut down.

Theater situation saved.

Win, win, and...

Yeah, there's still this: Shane Hott, with a big warm smile on his face that feels made just for me.

My blood hums a response, damn it.

I remind myself that he's an actor. His current job is to convince everyone on earth that he's into me. There could be paparazzi outside. We could be on video this very moment.

I'm five-eight—not petite for a woman—but he towers over me. I'm guessing six foot two, lean muscles and broad shoulders. He's wearing a pair of well-worn jeans with a thick leather belt, expensive loafers, and a soft-looking gray button-down. There's swagger in his walk, and I don't hate it.

This guy takes up space. He gives off heat. And he smells just the right amount like expensive, spicy aftershave.

"Let me buy you a drink," he says.

Alarm bells go off. In my mind, we would conduct all wedding-related business while sitting on opposite sides of a large table, preferably with chaperones present. But now he's gesturing at the Depot Hotel's bar—a series of closely placed stools—and, worse, I'm following him.

Before I drove here, I found myself deliberating over what top to wear. In exasperation with myself, I chose one of my oldest, rattiest T-shirts—and shoved my makeup bag into a drawer. I'm not doing makeup and costume for this guy.

Now I'm regretting it a little because the two of us are in public, him looking like his clothes were tailored onto him by the costume department just before he walked in...and me. And if there really *is* a paparazzo lurking nearby, it's going to be an embarrassing photo or video.

Fingers crossed for a last few moments of privacy before the storm descends.

The bartender comes by, and I order myself a glass of red wine. Shane asks for a single malt, neat, and an order of chips and guac.

I notice the couple a few seats down from us are whispering. Is it about us?

I was middling famous when I was on *Bridge*. I got recognized in public and we had a strong, enthusiastic fan base, but it wasn't an *everywhere I went* thing.

Shane Hott is seriously famous.

They're probably whispering about us. I figure we have about three days max before the whole world knows we're together.

Which is what Shane wants. And I want what Shane wants because he's killed my two ugly birds for me.

The bartender sets our drinks and chips down. "So we need a cover story," I say. "How we met, how we fell in love, when and where and why you proposed. I was thinking it might be good if we said we knew each other from LA. Because that helps explain to people who know us how things happened so fast."

He rakes his fingers through his bed-head hair. "The only problem with that is that when I actually saw you for the first time, my sister-in-law Sonya was there."

Right. When we crossed paths in Hott Spot.

"But that's okay, right? If all your siblings know it's fake, presumably that includes her, too?"

"Sure, yeah." He runs a finger around the rim of his

glass. "Which is a good thing because that first time I saw you, when I recovered my ability to speak, I'm pretty sure I said, 'Who was *that*?'"

"What do you mean, when you recovered your ability to speak?"

I'm trying not to read into what he's just said, but—

He grins at me. "In case you haven't noticed, Ivy, you're gorgeous. I saw you and temporarily lost use of my words."

Flustered, I fumble my wine, almost spilling. "Uh, thanks. I think."

"It's definitely a compliment."

I'm blushing, which… I'd forgotten the hardest aspect of acting a romance line—that you have to play the part without losing track of the fact that you're playing a part. And Shane is a genius at the romantic lead. That's how he's made his millions and captivated the hearts of the world's women.

I have to keep my focus. We're crafting a narrative here. Writing a fictional love story. While on the most public of all stages: real life in the age of social media.

Shane takes a drink, his eyes meeting mine over the rim of his glass. "And then the second time I saw you, you were talking to my brother Quinn, and I got jealous. Like *wanting to kick the crap out of him* jealous."

"Ooh, I like that!" I say. "That's a great touch. People will love it. We need to add more details along those lines. It's the details that make the story believable."

His eyebrows scrunch together. "That's what actually *happened*," he says.

I let him enjoy his joke for a beat, then laugh. He doesn't join me. He just watches me steadily, his eyes taking in every inch of my face. It's unnerving…and I like it way too much.

"Ha ha ha," I say when he doesn't deliver the punch line.

He gives me a quizzical look, his brown eyes all innocence and long lashes. "Uh, okay? But we actually *did* meet that time. It was at the fundraiser for Hott Spot, and you went up to the desk to talk to Quinn—"

"Oh, yeah, Quinn!" I say. "He's basically my hero."

He scowls. "Why would you say that?"

"Wait, what's wrong with Quinn being my hero?"

His scowl deepens. "I didn't say anything was wrong with it. I just asked why."

"You asked why in a way that made it sound like—never mind. He's my hero because he developed the drug that gave us a couple of years of extra time with my father. My dad had ALS."

"Ivy. I'm so sorry."

"Thank you," I say. "It was a really tough time, and I still miss him a lot. But yeah. That's why I love Quinn."

"Got it," he says stiffly. "Yeah. Can't compete with that."

If I didn't know better, I'd think he was jealous *now*. But that's ridiculous, right?

"I mean, I'm fake marrying you, not him, right? So you fake won the fake competition for who's the better catch."

He gives me a look I can't read. "Right."

I nosh a few chips and guac, pondering our story. I'm enjoying this more than I was expecting to. It's like building a character's backstory in acting. "Okay, so did we have a *history* in LA?"

"A romantic history?"

"Yeah. Or...maybe we were just friends and both wanted more, but circumstances made it impossible. Like you were just this total player and I didn't think you wanted commitment..."

"Best to stick with the truth," he says dryly, tossing back a sizable slug of scotch.

"...and I was getting out of LA for good and you didn't think I wanted that lifestyle, so even though we were both pining for each other, we didn't act on it."

"Sounds suspiciously close to real life," he says. "Minus the pining part, of course."

"Of *course*," I echo. "But don't you think we should stick as close to reality as we can? Makes it easier not to screw up the story."

"Yeah. Definitely."

"So in LA we wanted to be together but felt like we couldn't...but when we met again, we—"

"—couldn't stay away from each other," he supplies.

"One thing led to another—"

"We fell fast," he says. "It was a whirlwind. All that pent-up sexual tension."

"Right." My cheeks are hot, probably from the wine. My body feels loose and flowy, the way it does when I'm doing improv or acting. Creativity flowing through, wild, buzzy energy. "And it just *worked*. Like, you know when you have that chemistry with someone—"

"—the kind where you can't keep your hands off each other—" he throws in.

"—where it's almost...electric," I finish.

His face is flushed, his eyes bright, pupils big, and we grin at each other—because this is fun. We're good together. It makes me wonder how it would be to act opposite him.

I mean, after all, that's what this is. The two of us acting opposite each other in a movie about two people who meet, fall in love, get married, and then realize the error of their ways.

All in just a few months.

"And then I realized I didn't want to go back to LA without you," he says.

"Wait," I say. "You mean you realized you didn't want to go back to LA at all. You wanted to stay here with me."

He raises his eyebrows. "Wouldn't it make more sense for you to come back to LA and pick up your acting career? And then we live happily ever after?"

I shake my head. "There's nothing to pick up. I hated LA. I hated television. I love small-town life and my theater company. That's why we have to break up. We have irreconcilable difference. You want *bright lights, big city*, fame and fortune, and I want—" I gesture around us. "This. We try to make it work with long distance and commuting, but I have trust issues and you have—"

"I have commitment issues," he says wryly.

I nod.

He finishes off his scotch. "I guess we know how our breakup goes down."

"I guess we do. Wow, though. Whiplash. From sexual ecstasy to an ugly breakup in under ten minutes."

"Ecstasy, huh? That's a lot for a guy to live up to." His mouth quirks in a smile, but his gaze holds mine, curious and warm.

I bet you could do it, I want to say, but better judgment

prevails—for the moment. Instead I reach for my wine glass and sip. Actually, gulp.

"Anything else we need to go over?" he asks.

"If we were friends in LA, we'd need to know some things about each other's lives, right? Friends, family, major career issues. Maybe we each give each other a quick rundown, and then we fill in the details as needed?"

"Makes sense," he says. "My quick and dirty is…four brothers, one sister. Parents divorced—Dad stayed in LA. Mom passed when I was sixteen. I felt like my mom and granddad hadn't given my dad a fair shake and went to LA to live with him, to see if he'd take me under his wing in Hollywood. He did, and the rest is history."

"Your dad's what, a director…?"

"He was an actor, then an actor/director, then a director/producer. Now mostly an executive producer."

I rack my brain for a guy named Hott of that description but can't come up with one.

"Peter Hadley," he says to my blank expression.

"Oh! I know who he is."

"Most people do."

"You don't have his last name."

"All the siblings took my mom and granddad's last name."

There's got to be more to that story, but for now we've got to get the facts down. "I guess I should know your brothers' first names, huh?"

He laughs. "Probably. Preston's the oldest. He's in finance. Married to a woman he met in college, Kali. Then me. Then Rhys—family law, basically divorce. Then Tuck —he was in personal security until recently, but—" He stops. "No one really knows what's going on with Tuck. But it doesn't seem like he's working right now. And then there's Quinn."

"Right, Quinn." I beam.

He scowls. "I'm the only brother you're supposed to be into."

"Makes sense, right? I obviously have a thing for actors."

"Right, you dated that Anthony Fesser guy."

"Fessa."

"I've met him." He crosses his arms. "He's a prick."

"Yeah." I sigh.

"You, uh, want to tell me about it?"

I consider it for a split second, then shake my head. "Nah. I have to be a lot drunker than this to tell my Anthony story."

He laughs at that. "That bad, huh? Guess I'm lucky I don't fall in love."

"What, like *never*?"

"Never." He punctuates it with a single shoulder shrug. "And believe me, I've tried. After one particularly gruesome attempt, which destroyed a really great friendship with a woman I genuinely cared about, I realized that I needed to *stop* trying because I was blowing up stuff that actually mattered to me—" He gestures from his head down to his chest. "It helped to decide I wasn't meant for relationships. It freed me up to chase career opportunities."

That's...sad but also not surprising to me, as someone who spent longer than I would have liked in that world. There were a lot of people who'd decided that *La La Land* had it right and you could have love or fame but not both.

"Enough about that, though." He waves it off.

I wonder if there's more to the story than he's telling. There would have to be, right? This is the first hint of the real Shane I've seen, and I'm dying to ask him more. But I don't because I'm sure he's had enough of people prying under his defenses. "Speaking of line of work, what about career stuff? You just wrapped the last *Crown of Spires* movie, and you're...now what?"

He leans back. "Looking for my next project. There are a few possibilities. My father, who's also my manager, really wants me to do one movie, but—I don't know, I have some other ideas." He sips his scotch. "Okay, so what about you? What do I need to know? One sister—"

"Nia. She has a girlfriend, Akemi, and they live together in Rush Creek. My mom lives in Tarragona, Spain, with her new husband, who owns a coffee shop there."

"Tarragona," he repeats. "Is she of Spanish descent?"

"Nope. Went on a vacation, fell for the guy who made her coffee every morning."

"Nice. Okay. Mom in Tarragona. And I know you lost your dad, but—anything about him I should know?"

"He grew up in Newark, New Jersey. My parents met while they were teaching together in Bend. What about yours?" I ask him.

"Probably should mention—the Hott kids have three different dads. Pres, Rhys, and I; Tuck and Quinn; and Hanna."

His coloring—dark hair, dark eyes, skin hinting at olive, very different from Quinn's reddish hair and light skin— suddenly makes sense. I nod. "Okay. I can remember that. I think."

"This is like learning lines. Which, luckily for both of us, I'm actually pretty good at."

I grin. "Me, too."

"We'll have to go deeper than this," he warns.

"Character-wise, you mean," I say.

"Character-wise," he echoes, and our eyes meet again. "Did you think I meant it another way?" One eyebrow goes up, a challenge.

Heat spears through me. My face flames.

This is just an act, I remind myself. *You know better than to lust after a costar.*

"Just clarifying," I say and look away.

When I look back, he's pulling out his wallet, intently not making eye contact with me. Probably a good thing.

"I gotta go," he says, tossing cash onto the bar. "I promised Hanna I'd stop by tonight and do a shift with my baby niece, Eloise, so she can get some sleep even though Easton's on a trip."

I reach for my purse, and he waves me off. "I've got this."

I don't protest. Even if this setup benefits me as much as him, it was his idea—and plus, if we were really together, I'd probably be letting him pay for me, given the disparity in our current incomes and the fact that we're—as far as the world knows—about to merge finances.

He stands up, and I'm struck again by the way his torso tapers from broad shoulders to trim waist, the power hinted at by the play of muscles under his expensive clothes. "We can pick this up again soon and fill in the blanks. And we're gonna need to out ourselves on social media. I'm thinking we should get something up soon, something that looks like we didn't mean for it to get out there."

"Like what?" I ask.

"Video of me leaving your house would probably do it," he says. "And then I can have someone 'accidentally' leak it to this paparazzo who owes me a favor. That way we can control the timing."

"I could get my sister to film that," I say. "Since she already knows the whole scoop."

"That would work."

"How about tomorrow morning at nine. Like you're sneaking out?"

He gives me an eyebrow raise. "And I don't even get to sleep in your bed for my trouble?"

I blush and, to cover my confusion, text my sister.

Ivy: Want to meet Shane Hott?

Nia: Where? When?

Ivy: Tomorrow at nine. My place.

Nia: With bells on, sister.

I turn back to find Shane watching me, his expression inscrutable.

"We're on," I tell him. "Tomorrow, nine, my place. I'll text you the address."

He nods.

"Uh," I say. "I guess we have to—what? Hug? Something?"

"Works for me," he says, and suddenly, before I can

brace myself properly, I'm wrapped in muscular arms and pressed against a strong, lean body.

Whoa.

He kisses my hair and releases me.

"Bye, babe," he says.

He strides toward the elevator, leaving behind the scent of expensive aftershave and me—a limp, noodly, tingly puddle of *holy shit what just happened to me.*

10

IVY

When we converge on my house the next morning, Nia plays it way more cool than I was expecting her to. She barely fangirls at all. She just shakes Shane's hand, smiles at him, and then listens to his instructions about where to stand—the bushes—and how to film us—"Like you're trying really hard not to be seen. It has to be that way to be believable," he explains.

"You stand just inside the door," he tells me, pointing. "With the door open."

We set up like we're saying goodbye as he leaves.

"Come close," he says.

I hesitate. Not because I don't want to be close to Shane Hott, but because I want it a little too much. Last night's hug was a reminder of just how good it feels to be a) held and b) held by a guy whose body is sculpted for women's admiration.

I admired.

I admired and tingled for several hours afterward.

Falling asleep required a five-fingered trick to release the tension. I tried not to explicitly fantasize about Shane...

And failed.

"I'm only going to touch your hand," he says. Kindly, since I've been standing here frozen for an indecent amount of time.

It's not the possibility of touching that has me off-balance. It's the fact that our faces are inches apart and his breath is brushing my skin. I can smell not just aftershave and deodorant and shampoo and toothpaste but something so essentially him that it must be the scent of his skin. I catch myself drifting closer, leaning in, and pull back to the distance he set us at.

He takes my hand. My breath stutters, and I hope it's subtler than it sounds.

"You good?" he calls to Nia. "Start filming."

Shane pulls slowly away from me, his fingers sliding along mine, the friction starting a beat of desire between my legs. And those are just his fingers. Imagine...

No. Don't imagine!

He breaks contact finally, his hand dropping to his side. "I'll see you soon," he says. He starts a slow lope to the curb. Looking back at me once. Twice. Longingly.

"Cut," he calls as he reaches his car.

"Got it!" Nia says. "It looks good!"

He takes the phone from her, and we watch the video.

If I didn't know better, I'd totally buy it. We look like we've spent an epic night together and now we're saying goodbye, both so loath to let the other go we can barely stand to let our fingers slip apart.

"We're good together," he says offhandedly.

He doesn't mean it *that* way. He doesn't mean it that way.

If I say it enough times, I will definitely believe it.

I've acted a lot of romantic scenes. I'm a trained professional. I'm good with a lot of men.

And yet: Shane's hand around mine did something decidedly unprofessional to my heart rate. As did the way he gazed into my eyes.

He's a thoroughly believable romantic hero.

I definitely should never watch the spire sex scene.

"You know what we should do?" Nia says, eyes opening wide. "We should totally film your proposal! That would definitely permanently shut down Anthony—"

"Nia," I say sharply.

"Oh," she says, clapping a hand to her mouth and looking from me to Shane. "I assumed—"

He's looking at both of us, waiting for an explanation.

"I didn't tell you this because it didn't seem relevant," I admit to him. "But part of why I agreed to do this is because my ex tried to trap me into a PR marriage with him by filming himself doing this whole elaborate proposal to me—"

"He *what*?"

Shane Hott, easygoing, chill, loved by all, has disappeared, and in his place is a towering hostile man-god who looks like he would break Anthony over his knee. And I'm not gonna lie, I like it.

"It's fine," I say because although the angry man-god is hot and I adore the idea of Anthony squealing for mercy, I don't really want Shane to give my asshole ex the time of day. I wave my hand. "I turned him down by saying I was already engaged."

Shane's shoulders slowly relax, his jaw loosening. "Good," he says. "Because that's— I can't even— If he tries anything like that again, you tell me, okay?"

Well, well, well, what do we have here? It's not like he has to play a role for Nia's sake; she knows what's going on. But this is definitely Shane the Protector. He reminds me of his counterpart in *Crown of Spires*, all swagger and alpha posturing. And I madly, deeply love it.

"Uh, yeah," I say. "Okay."

"And staging a proposal—let me think about that," he says to Nia. "That's a great idea."

When Shane's gone, my sister dissolves into squeeing. "Omigod, omigod, omigod. He's, like, so larger than life and *good looking* and *fierce*. And I don't even want to fuck him. I just want to stare at him." She eyes me. "What? Why are you so quiet? You *do*. You want to—"

"Hush! Nia!"

She raises an eyebrow. "No one would blame you! That *I'll break his face for you* thing was *hot*. And duh, obviously, you need to try out spire sex with the lord of the skies."

"I haven't even watched that scene yet!"

Now it's both eyebrows, and she's having trouble hiding her smile. "But you did watch the first movie." It's not really a question, not with that smirk.

"It seemed like important research."

"Has Shane watched *Bridge*?" she asks.

"Not relevant!"

"So, so relevant. Next time you see him, you have to ask

him if he's jerked off to Oriana getting boned in the engine room."

"There is absolutely no way I'm going to ask—"

"Kidding, Ivy, *kidding*."

I roll my eyes and slump against the doorframe. I have zero desire to admit it, but the fact that Shane watched some of my show, might even have watched the infamous engine-room scene, causes my skin to glow with heat. In general, I never want anyone to confuse me with Oriana, but somehow this is different. Maybe because Shane is an actor, too, and knows the difference between me in real life and me on-screen.

He'd get to see you naked. Maybe pause the scene and rewatch. Reach for his belt buckle and the zipper under it.

What's behind that zipper?

"Ivy?"

"Sorry," I say. "Was thinking about—"

"Sex hundreds of feet off the ground? While tied to a spire?"

"Shut. It. Shane and I are not having sex—on a spire or anywhere. His motives for doing this whole fake marriage are even purer than mine. And everyone wins if we pull this off."

"Which does not preclude your having sex with him," she points out.

"No, but having sex with him would make this so, so much messier. Right now it's an acting job. A business contract. Sex would add the mother of all swerve to the mix."

Her smile drops away. "Okay. I can see that. So you're really doing this, huh?"

"Seems like it."

She crosses her arms. "You better get one hell of a proposal on video. If you're going to get rid of losers, users, and trolls—Anthony foremost among them—you need the lord of the skies to stake his claim and show the world how it's done."

I raise my eyebrows. "No pressure on him."

"I mean, you're getting *married* to save his family's business. The least he can do is propose like a boss."

"Mmm, good point," I say. "I'll tell him so."

She grins. "Hey. Are you letting Mom in on the secret?"

I squeeze my eyes shut. I've been trying not to think about my mother, on the other side of the Atlantic from my shenanigans. "I was hoping I could maybe get away with not telling her about the engagement at all?"

Nia tilts her head, considering. "What happens if she finds out? She does read American news."

"She quit after we pointed out that it made her miserable."

"True. You could not tell her for now, and if she finds out, you could do triage then." She chuckles. "I still think it's pretty rich. You've been hiding out for years, and now you're going public with a big, fat fake wedding. You've been avoiding players and liars, and now you're going to spend months with a guy who's obviously fine being both."

"At least what you see is what you get with Shane," I point out. "I already know he's a player, and right now we're both liars."

That makes this totally different from things with Anthony, who let me think he was a good guy who loved me, when in fact he was a Hollywood user.

We both mull that for a moment. "There is that," she says. "And maybe this'll be good for you. Maybe getting back in the public eye will scare up some TV or film opportunities."

"I don't want TV or film opportunities. You know that."

She gives me a long, hard look.

"I don't! If I wanted them, I'd be pursuing them."

"Okay." She shrugs. "I got it. You don't want sex with Shane Hott, and you don't want to act in film or TV again."

I didn't say I don't want sex with Shane Hott. "I love my life here."

"I love your life here, too," she says and wraps an arm around my shoulder. "Just tell me how I can help."

When she lets me go, I watch her walk down my front path, between the two sides of my garden, to her car. I wave and slip back into the house.

I stand inside the door, right where I stood a moment ago with Shane's big, warm hand wrapped tightly around mine.

What's weird is that even though I told Nia the truth, the whole truth, and nothing but the truth, my chest still aches like I've told a lie.

11

SHANE

"So," I say. "I, um—I'm going to propose to my girlfriend."

Five Hott siblings and Sonya turn to me in a movement so coordinated it could have been choreographed.

We're all gathered at Hanna and Easton's house to celebrate Eloise's christening earlier this morning. It was the first time all six Hott siblings were under the same church roof since Preston was in high school. We didn't even all make it for Hanna's wedding, which is still a source of shame to those of us who thought at the time that we had more pressing engagements. (Read: Me. I was filming, but I still regret not telling my director to put it on ice so I could watch my baby sister walk down the aisle.)

After the christening, the Wilders and the Hotts came back to the house, the little bungalow bursting at the seams with all the combined energy.

Easton cooked up a giant batch of his family's spaghetti, people brought side dishes and desserts, and several giant ice tubs overflowed with drinks. We passed baby Eloise from arms to arms, everyone cooing over her. Meanwhile the Wilder cousins organized themselves into a surprisingly civilized and fair game of wiffle ball, loosely overseen by various Wilder brothers and their wives and girlfriends, and chased by Gabe's and Sonya's dogs.

Now, though, the party's broken up, leaving just Hotts, Hanna's husband Easton, Quinn's wife Sonya, and Sonya's dog Gus, who looks like a Dr. Seuss character and adores Eloise so much that he'll sit on his haunches next to her swing, watching her sleep and panting at the amount of restraint required not to lick every inch of her.

We're all gathered in the kitchen, helping with cleanup.

Or, well, that was what they were doing a moment ago, until my *I'm proposing* bombshell. Now they're all staring at me, wide-eyed, frozen in mid-motion, dishes and silverware and baby-bottle parts in hand.

Then Rhys snorts and Preston bursts out laughing.

"Oh my God," Rhys says. "That's actually brilliant! Why didn't any of us think of that before?"

"Let me guess," Preston says. "She's *a celebrity*."

It's obvious that I couldn't have met someone, fallen in love, and decided to get married since the last time we were all together. But it still galls me a tiny bit that the idea is so absurd that they assume I have to be faking it for the will.

I mean, even if I *am* faking it for the will.

And even if I've never nurtured the *slightest* thought that marriage might be for me.

"Obviously she's a celebrity," Rhys says. "Everyone in Shane's life is basically a celebrity."

"We're not," Hanna points out.

"I'm just saying it was inevitable that when Shane got engaged, it would be to a celebrity."

Hanna's eyebrows draw together. "But Shane's not *really* getting engaged. He's f—"

"*Yes, he is,*" Rhys interrupts crisply. He winks at me. "Han. Think about it this way. It's a basic law tactic. Attorneys don't ask clients to answer questions they don't want to know the answers to because then they won't have to actually *lie*. Plausible deniability. If he just tells us he's getting engaged, we can take it as gospel that he is and pass that along to everyone else. Like Weggers. Shane *is* getting engaged. He just told us so."

My sister's gaze swings to me. "Is that how it is?"

Easton closes a cabinet and joins her, tugging her to his side. "He can't answer that," he murmurs to her. "That's the whole point."

"Ohhhhhhhh," she says.

He gives her a fond look and kisses her cheek, mussing her short hair.

Damn. I wish I'd thought of this idea myself. I like Rhys's plausible-deniability reasoning. This way I don't have to make my siblings outright lie for me.

"So who is she?" Easton asks me.

"I've actually known her a while." Might as well practice the story, if we're going to play this Rhys's way.

"Of course you have," Hanna says. "And we all knew about her." She winks exaggeratedly at me.

I seriously hope she'll be a more convincing liar by the time we have to meet with Weggers.

"I definitely did," Preston says, already in the flow. "You mentioned her to me way back when you first met her. I could tell from the way you talked about her that this one was different."

I probably shouldn't be surprised that Preston, whose parentage is the same as mine, can act. Or that he catches on quickly. A guy who rose meteorically in New York finance is bound to learn to play the game fast.

"That was probably when we were still just friends," I say. "When she thought I was just a player and she was leaving LA, so I didn't even feel like I could make a move. But then I was here working on the January and Tobias wedding and we ran into each other again and *blam*."

Actually, that's not a bad description of the feeling I had the first time I crossed paths with Ivy.

"So convenient," Tucker mutters. That's about all we get out of him these days. No one knows exactly what's going on with him, and he won't discuss it. If you ask if he's okay, he shrugs and says he's fine.

"How did you two meet originally?" Rhys wants to know.

"I first met her in LA at a party with mutual friends. We hit it off, met for coffee to talk shop—"

Ivy and I worked out a story that would be hard to refute. Our idea was that plenty of people can say they didn't know we knew each other, but no one can prove we didn't. As long as we don't tell an outright lie, Weggers won't have anything on us.

"—anyway, we became friends. It would've been more, but she knew I wasn't relationship material and kept me at arm's length. Then things blew up with her and she ended up coming to Rush Creek to get away from LA. She'd quit acting and I lost touch with her, and then—blam—I ran into her at Hott Spot. And it was—"

It's convenient not to have to lie about this part. "It was pretty instant, for me at least. I was like, *I'm not letting this woman get away again.*"

My voice gets husky. I'd like to say it's because I'm a brilliant actor, but it's actually because I accidentally let myself think about Ivy. The sunshine-yellow hair and the big brown eyes, the willowy curves and the wry smile.

And that fucking hug the other night.

What was I thinking?

I was thinking, *I'm a hugger. I hug women all the time. And it doesn't usually make me need to go home and bang my right hand like it's going out of style.*

"Sonya and Quinn know her," I say because I definitely need a change of topic. "Her dad took Quinn's drug."

"You're talking about Eva. Ivy," Quinn says.

"Yeah."

His eyes probe mine, and I have to look away because it's like he can see straight through me. I have the strangest thought.

He's going to out me.

But I don't mean he's going to tell them—and Weggers —that none of my avowed feelings for Ivy are real.

I mean he's going to tell them that I actually like her.

Which, let's be straight about this, I do.

She's brave, for one thing, because you have to have guts to take this on. And she's big hearted, going to these lengths to help a bunch of struggling theater kids.

She's incredibly game and quick witted. When we were

brainstorming our story together, it was the best kind of collaboration, when you feel like you're right in someone else's head. Like your ideas and their ideas get wrapped up together.

And I like that she knows what she wants. A job she loves, a house, a garden, and people she trusts.

For a split second, I wanted to volunteer. *Me! Me! Pick me!*

Obviously I can't actually volunteer to be a person Ivy can trust. My reputation speaks for itself. I'm more likely to be the talk of the town in the worst possible way than the guy you call because you need someone you can depend on.

Still, for just a second, I wanted it.

When I look back at Quinn and company, all of my siblings—and Easton and Sonya—are staring at me. I realize I lost my focus there for a second. Who knows what my face did while I wasn't paying attention?

Quinn's staring hardest. He opens his mouth.

Before he can say anything else, though, Sonya lets out a cry of dismay.

"Gus!"

Her dog has been busy while we were all otherwise engaged. He nosed into Eloise's diaper bag and managed to root out three of her pacifiers, and now he's sitting on the floor with the pacis between his front paws, licking them affectionately.

Sonya snatches all three pacifiers away from Gus and, nose wrinkled, hands them to Easton for washing. Gus barks in protest, then gets up and settles at Hanna's feet, panting up at Eloise in her arms.

In the flurry, Quinn seems to have forgotten about my

romantic life, but Hanna hasn't. "So, tell us. Where, when, how—all the deets."

"I want us to get married right away," I say.

I mean, we could dispense with the theatrics here, but might as well go through the ritual.

"We've known each other a long time, and once we realized how compatible we are, you know—"

"Sexually?" Preston supplies, and Hanna scrunches her face like she smells something bad.

"Yeah," I sigh. "Once we figured that out, it was like that *When Harry Met Sally* thing. When you realize you want to spend the rest of your life with someone, you want the rest of your life to start as soon as possible. So I'm going to ask her to marry me, and if you still have that Tobuary wedding date available, we'll take that."

"Of course you will," Tucker mutters.

"Dude," Rhys says. "Show a little respect here. You're in the presence of True Love." He flicks me a glance, as if to say, *Isn't this the most absurd thing you and I have ever heard?*

"I haven't canceled all the vendors yet," Hanna says. "We should keep whatever we can and only change what you two feel strongly about. Because that's a really short time frame. Are you going to do evites?"

I hadn't given it a millisecond of thought, but I nod. "And we'll keep it on the small side, since we know it's incredibly last minute."

"You'll all be at the wedding, right?" Hanna asks, panning her gaze around to all my brothers.

It's not really a question. It's pretty obvious that to make this convincing, we all have to play our parts.

Preston and Rhys say they can come back then, and Tucker grunts in a way that's probably a yes.

"Kali, too!" Hanna tells Preston. "We miss her. Tell her she has to take work off."

For no particular reason, my eyes are on Preston's face when Hanna says that, so I see what almost no one else sees: all the color leaving his face.

"Uh, I'm pretty sure she has a conference then," he says, voice strained. "Ninety percent sure."

"I've got Friday morning free if you want to come in for your first meeting then," Hanna says.

"I have to check with Ivy—"

"Where *is* Ivy?" Hanna asks.

"She and I thought given how fast this all happened that it would be better for me to tell you all first before you meet her."

"I would have thought she'd be here. Such an important day. Such a big party," my sister needles.

"She didn't want to overshadow Eloise's big day," I toss back.

"What a sweetheart," Hanna says dryly.

It's going to be a long month.

"And, uh, I need some help with something else," I say.

Eyebrows rise.

"I need a *really* good proposal."

12

IVY

I'm eating breakfast the next morning—granola and milk—when Shane shows up at my front door. He's wearing jeans, a soft sage-green T-shirt, and a pair of expensive-looking suede tennis shoes.

It's not so much the clothes themselves, though, as the way they fit his strong, muscular body. He leans casually against one pillar of my porch, hands shoved into his pockets, and my mouth goes dry.

"Uh, hey?" I say.

"Sorry to just show up like this." Although he doesn't look sorry. He looks the way Shane Hott always looks, accustomed to getting his own way, comfortable in his own skin, at ease in the world. "But it occurred to me we should say as little in text as possible, so our texts don't become something Weggers can use against me later."

"Makes sense." I don't point out that he could have called, because I'm actually delighted to see him. Which I hate, to be honest. And perhaps because of that, I'm still lingering on my side of the door, not quite opening it all the way to him—like my front door is any kind of shield against Shane's bigger-than-life Hottness.

"I thought we could plan the proposal."

"Ohh," I say. "Yeah. Okay. Come on in."

He follows me inside. "Really cute place," he says, looking around.

My house is a twelve-hundred-square-foot bungalow, cozy as a blanket. My couches were Craigslist specials, my rugs hand-me-downs from late relatives, my furniture garage- and estate-sale finds. I bought it with the last of my *Bridge* earnings, it's all been assembled with love, and I adore every piece—but suddenly I'm self-conscious. I'm betting he lives in a ten-thousand-square-foot Hollywood mansion.

But if he's judging my stuff, he definitely doesn't show it. "Feels really homey. I can never get my place to feel like this. Mine feels..." He sighs. "Sterile."

I raise my eyebrows. "You could always tell your designer that you want to redo it, 'yard-sale chic.'"

He laughs, eyes flashing to my face in appreciation, but doesn't deny that he has a designer at his beck and call. "Do you think that would actually work?"

"I mean, if they're any good and you said you wanted something 'cozier' or 'homier,' yeah, probably."

He looks around. "Maybe I'll try it. I just want it to feel like a home, instead of...I don't know. A sound stage for a movie set in a Hollywood mansion."

"Money can't buy you love, huh?"

"Ha, no," he says, but his laugh sounds hollow, and our eyes meet, a flash of sympathy arcing between us. Two people who know that fame and fortune can feel as empty as that laugh.

"Uh, can I get you something to drink? Coffee, tea, kombucha, a green smoothie with kale and chia seeds?"

He narrows his eyes at me. "Are you making fun of me?"

"I'm making fun of Hollywood. Tell me I'm wrong."

"I hate kombucha."

"But you do drink green smoothies. And eat Buddha bowls."

He sighs.

"I have hummus and carrots," I say. "I could run to the store for some chia seeds."

He groans.

"Or..." I go to the pantry. "I've got a couple of scones left from a batch I baked."

"My trainer will never speak to me again if I eat one of those."

"What they don't know can't hurt them," I point out.

He laughs. "You've got a point there. Scones, please."

I bring out a plate and set the scones on my coffee table, a punched metal top with reclaimed-wood legs made by a guy appropriately named Sawyer who sells upcycled wood furniture online.

"So. You want to propose."

I say it super casually, but I'm still having moments here and there of not being able to believe this is actually my *life*. Shane Hott is here to *plan the proposal we're staging.*

He chuckles. "Yeah. I want to propose. And I want to upstage that dick Anthony Fessa. You good with that?"

I grin. "I'm beyond good with that."

"How did he propose?" He tilts his head. "If you don't

mind telling me. I know you said you had to be drunk to tell me about him."

I laugh. "Not the proposal. That's a comedy routine. First of all, he hired a band to play 'All You Need Is Love.'"

"Very shades of *Love Actually*," he says, rolling his eyes.

"And then he—" I close my eyes.

"That bad?"

I sigh. "How many *Bridge* episodes did you watch?"

"Just the first five."

"Well, spoiler alert—Oriana knows how to have a good time." I'm blushing.

"If you're alluding to the engine-bay scene—"

"So you do know about it."

"People—men—don't seem to be able to talk about the show without mentioning that scene." In response to my raised eyebrows and deepening blush, he says, "I didn't watch it."

"Well. Maybe...don't."

He smirks. "We'll see about that."

"Just know that if you watch that scene, I'm going to watch your apparently epic spire scene."

"Is that supposed to be a deterrent?" he teases, voice low and honey edged. "That scene definitely shows me in my best light."

"Meaning in the dark?" I tease back, and he grins, crinkles forming around his eyes, dimples dropping in to his cheeks.

"Watch away," he says, waving his hand. "I'll be curious what you think. But you were saying...?"

"There's the infamous engine-bay scene, and then there's this other scene..."

I don't want to say it.

"'Fill me up with babies'?" he suggests, the corners of his mouth tilting up.

"Good to know I don't have any secrets."

"Engine Girl, neither of us has any secrets."

I roll my eyes at the nickname. "I loathe that 'fill me up with babies and take me away from the loneliness at the end of the universe' monologue. And Anthony, who has no sense of irony, used it in the proposal."

"Asshole," he growls, and I have to pretend to myself that I don't feel that growl in the most sensitive parts of my body. "Do you get this kind of bullshit a lot?"

"I mean, fans can definitely cross the line. Overall I think I've been pretty lucky. No restraining orders or anything. Oriana's got her followers, but we were still a little bit of a cult show. Not mainstream enough to bring out the stalkers in droves."

He's shaking his head, but it's shared aggravation, not shock. I have the feeling that I can't tell Shane Hott anything he doesn't already know about the perils of fame. "Some of the fan shenanigans are really bad," he says.

"You, too?"

"Oh yeah. But I know it's different for men. I'm glad it hasn't been in restraining-order territory for you." He leans back on the couch and stretches out his legs. "So you said you watched *Crown of Spires*?"

"I only watched the first one." I bite my lip. "I heard about your famous scene from my sister."

He scowls. "Just so you know, there is *nothing* sexy about pretending to be in the throes of passion while suspended against a green screen on wires."

I laugh. "I can only imagine."

"And I suspect you think there is nothing sexy about pretending to have sex while cameras circle you and highly paid consultants order you around so no one's consent rights get violated..."

I blink, surprised. "No." It's a strange sensation, to be around someone who gets it. For two people who don't know each other at all, we already know a lot about each other.

Now, of course, I'm wondering what *is* sexy to Shane Hott?

And is he wondering what's sexy to me?

He leans in, his eyes on my mouth, and I strongly suspect he is. Then, like he's suddenly realized where we are and what we're supposed to be doing, he sits up straight and says, "So. Proposal. I'm thinking we do it in character."

"What, like you're Mavryx and I'm Lady Whatserface?"

He laughs at that. "No. I'm Mavryx, and you're *Oriana*."

I hesitate.

"I know," he says. "I don't love it when people confuse me and Mavryx, either, but in this case? I think it'll get the fans really excited—and that's what we need."

"But Mavryx and Oriana don't even exist in the same...world?"

"Do you trust me?"

"Not at all."

That makes him laugh.

"Let me be more specific. Would you trust me to stage the best public marriage proposal you've ever gotten?"

"Better than Anthony's?"

"Promise. This marriage proposal will guarantee that Anthony's stays on ice for all eternity."

I search his face. He's been honest with me so far. Plus, he exudes a deep confidence, bordering on cockiness, and I'll admit it: I want to know what it would feel like to put myself in his hands.

Not literally, of course.

But I could let him take the lead on this. See where it goes.

I nod, and he pumps a fist.

"Don't make me regret this," I warn.

"I won't," he says.

I don't completely believe him.

13

IVY

S hane whips his phone out.

"Who are you texting?" I ask.

"You said you trusted me."

"I didn't *mean* it."

He rolls his eyes at me.

"Just tell me?" I plead.

"I'm texting Quinn's wife. Sonya. I need her to mobilize her posse."

"Her—posse?"

"Just take my word for it. And text me your sister's number, too."

"My sister's—"

"She's the same size as you, right?"

Nia and I are exactly the same size, which has always been handy for the purposes of borrowing clothes. "Right," I say. "Can I ask what you're up to?"

"Nope," he says. "Just text me her number."

"Does Sonya know we're fake?"

He grimaces. "Uh. It's complicated."

I laugh. "Everything about this situation is complicated."

"My brother Rhys wants me to do this plausible-deniability thing where we talk about it like it's real. And it makes sense. We talk about it like it's real, we text about it like it's real, and then we're a lot less likely to fuck up when it matters."

"Makes sense," I say slowly.

"So technically I haven't *said* it's fake. But my whole family knows it's fake, because it's obvious that it's fake, because they know I'm not the kind of guy who gets married. I'm just not a guy who sticks."

That's probably true, at least if you believe the way he's portrayed in the press. Every time he appears, it's with a different woman, and the media loves to make a big deal about the revolving door.

Not a guy who sticks.

It's a good reminder to the part of me that finds him increasingly appealing as we spend more time together.

Shane Hott is *not* an eligible bachelor. He's not husband material. He's a guy who doesn't stick.

"Okay, well, make sure you tell Nia about the plausible-deniability thing, too," I say, pointing at his phone.

"Will do. And I think Sonya's bringing a couple friends, so we'll have to stay in character anyway. The story we're going with is that I already proposed to you in private, and now we're filming an internet-worthy proposal for our fans."

"So much for keeping things simple," I goad him. "None of this is gonna come back to bite us in the ass or anything."

He smiles wryly. "We've got this. Have faith."

"Famous last words."

It doesn't take long before there's a knock at my door. Shane opens it and hugs a dark-haired woman toting shopping bags, then introduces us. "Sonya, this is my fiancée, Ivy."

"I know Ivy!" Sonya says, beaming. "She's a beloved customer at Hott Spot."

Even though I know what she said is just good customer service, her praise makes me blush. Sometimes you feel like just a name in an appointment book, but the way Sonya's smiling at me suggests she means what she says.

"So," she says, taking my hands in hers. "You're Shane's fiancée! Welcome to the family."

Did she just wink at me? I blinked and missed it. Her gaze is curious but not judgmental, and I remind myself that she and Quinn probably got together because of a clause in the Hott will. I need to ask Shane what happened between them.

Regardless, it looks like she has my back—and I'm grateful for that.

"Thank you," I say, and we smile at each other.

She sets down her shopping bags in the kitchen and turns to me.

"Let's start with eyebrows." She examines them, smoothing them with slim, cool fingers. I eye her own hair and makeup, which are flawless—subtle natural color on her olive skin, hair that she ironed into perfect ringlets. Plus I love her outfit, a pair of flowy pants and a wrap blouse that emphasize her narrow waist and hourglass curves.

"I'll be back," Shane says.

"Where are you going?" I ask him.

"I have some things I need to get."

I watch his denim-clad muscular ass exit my front door.

"They don't call them the Hott brothers for nothing," Sonya murmurs, following my gaze, and I laugh.

She leads me into the kitchen, and I turn myself willingly over to her. She's gentle and her hands are soft and vanilla scented, and I feel like I'm having a spa day in my own house.

Just as Sonya finishes my eyebrows and puts away her wax pot, two more women show up. One has shoulder-length multicolored hair and is wearing a miniskirt with fishnet stockings and a crocheted black vest over a long-sleeved black tee. "Reggie," she says, shaking my hand. "I'm on hair."

"I'm Bella," says the other. She's matronly and a little older than her companions, with silvery hair and a warm smile. "Makeup."

I have to assume Reggie and Bella think Shane and I are together for real. So it's time to be fully in character.

I focus on glowing. And looking giddy. As any woman should when she's about to marry Shane Hott. It's actually not difficult because I'm feeling warm and flushed and oddly happy.

"Should I start on hair?" Reggie asks Sonya.

Her brow creases. "Normally I'd say yes. But in this case I think hair's going to be a messy bun, so we should get her dressed first."

Outside, a car engine draws near. Bella goes to the window. "Shane's back," she says. "Give me the bag with his stuff. Do you have a guest room or something we could use?"

"Second door on the left once you're up the stairs," I tell her.

Sonya hands a shopping bag to Bella, who disappears. A moment later, I hear Shane's rich, warm laugh, and footsteps pound up my stairs.

"What's in Shane's bag?" I ask.

"You'll find out," Sonya says with a laugh. "Bella and I made the rounds of all our friends' houses this morning, and that bag is the fruit of our labors."

I'm dying of curiosity.

Just then the doorbell rings again. The door swings open and Nia stands there.

"I'm here!" she announces.

"Excellent," Sonya says.

"Sorry I'm late," she tells me. "Sonya sent me on a mission, and it was surprisingly challenging." She holds out a small blue plastic shopping bag, and Sonya takes it from her.

She dumps the contents onto the table, then tosses a scrap of fabric at me. My reflexes kick in and I catch it right before it hits me in the face. At first I think it's a bra; then I realize it's nominally a shirt. A tiny bandeau top, ivory floral, ruched and smocked and beyond adorable.

"What's this?"

"Your top," Nia says. "I went to four stores in Bend before I found it."

"Wait, what?'

Sonya dumps the contents of the other shopping bag

onto the kitchen table and tugs something free. "It's to wear with these."

She holds up something very...denim. "I wore these last year for Halloween."

"What were you? A sexy mechanic?"

"I was Oriana," she says with sheepish grin. "Last year. Reggie was Oriana the year before that."

"Wait. You watched *Bridge*?"

"I love *Bridge*," she says.

"Why didn't you say something?"

"Because I didn't want to be all awkward and fangirl-y."

My whole chest is a big, warm *awwwwww*, but I just say, quietly, "Thank you."

"Any time." She hands me the overalls. "We all love the show. But no one needs someone fawning over them."

"No," I agree. "No one does."

I meet my sister's eyes, and she smiles at me, as if to say, *See? There are a lot of good people out there.*

Nia's right, and I need to give the adults of Rush Creek as much credit as I've given their kids.

I hold up the overalls. I hate to admit it, but they're perfect. They're soft and distressed, generously torn in places.

"Let's see them on you," Sonya says.

I duck into the small bath and tug the top on. It fits perfectly, thanks to Nia's sizing efforts. Then I slip into the overalls. With the top, they're the same smoking-hot combination of innocent and earthy that got Oriana and me in trouble to begin with.

I step out of the bathroom. "I don't know."

"Oh my God, yes!" Sonya cries.

Nia nods decisively. "Definitely. You look really hot. Can I have that whole outfit when you're done with it?"

We all laugh.

Nia steps closer, unfastening one strap of my overalls, letting it dangle. I try to refasten it, but Sonya says, "Leave it."

Bella trots back into the kitchen, looking pleased with herself. "Mission accomplished," she says, grinning. "This is fun. Can we move to LA and costume movie stars all the time?"

An idea hits me. "You could stay right here in Rush Creek and help out Nia and me with costuming at the theater. And hair and makeup, if you're interested."

"I would love that!" she says, beaming.

"That sounds like so much fun," Sonya says. "If I'd known you needed volunteers, I would have been there in a heartbeat."

"Me three," Reggie pipes up.

"Oh, we can always use volunteers," I say. "But we also have a small stipend for it!"

Sonya waves that away. "Save it for something else. I'd do this for fun any time."

She pulls up a photo on her phone screen and hands it to Reggie. "Hair like this," she says.

The other woman studies the screen and nods. "You got it, boss."

She works on my hair while Sonya fusses over my face. Just as they finish up, Shane calls down from upstairs.

"You ready for me?"

Something in my chest squeezes at the sound of his

voice. I'm definitely *not* ready for the force of nature that is Shane Hott.

"Yup," Sonya calls back. She hustles me into the bathroom so I can look at myself in the mirror.

Oriana looks back at me. Glowing porcelain skin, pink cheeks, red lips, bun just-out-of-bed chic. Breasts barely contained by the little top, overalls unfastened like I'm two seconds from getting boned in the engine room.

There are footfalls on the stairs. I step out of the bathroom and feast my eyes on the sight confronting me.

A fae lord—towering, gorgeous, bare-chested, and winged—steps into my kitchen. His shoulders barely clear the doorway. His hair is long and thick, swept back from his face, tucked behind pointed ears. A jeweled crown sits low on his head. His mouth is wide, lush, and a deep red. His lashes are long and thick, his eyes slightly uptilted, cat-like.

He's wearing black breeches, and two thick leather straps crisscross his smooth, tanned torso and rippling abs. A dusting of dark hair peeks through the cut-out leather at the center of his chest.

He is the most beautiful creature I have ever seen or imagined.

His eyes rake over my costume.

"Holy shit," he says. "I didn't think I was into sexy-mechanic kink, but you just broke my brain."

I go hot all over.

Shane Hott thinks I'm sexy.

I broke his brain.

That makes two of us.

I try to keep my gaze from dropping to the fly of his breeches—I desperately want to know if his brain is the only thing with an opinion of my costume—but I fail. And I don't know if there's some kind of magic that works when you put an actor in breeches, but there is *definitely* some kind of magic going on behind that fly, and I want a piece of it.

"You two are adorable!" Sonya says. "We need a *Crown of Spires*/*Bridge* crossover event."

"There's something missing," Shane muses.

"On it," Reggie says, reaching into her purse and coming out with something that looks like a black Chap-Stick. "Stole this from my hot firefighter boyfriend. He plays every form of rec-league sportsball known to man and wears the under-eye grease stuff to keep the sunlight out so he can catch sportsballs. Totally over the top, but somehow still hot AF?" She rolls her eyes and holds out the greasepaint. "Shane, you want to do the honors?"

Whoops.

Of course she'd think Shane should do it. She thinks Shane and I are actually a couple. Putting greasepaint on your fiancée is no big deal—probably less weird than painting it on a friend you just met an hour ago.

I send my sister a pleading look, but she shakes her head slightly. She's right—enough people already know or suspect that this is fake. I need to put on my big girl pants and play my role.

Reggie sets the makeup stick in Shane's palm. He opens it and steps closer to me. He's so close I can smell mint and feel his breath on my face. My heart pounds. He puts a hand on my cheek, his thumb inches from my mouth. Tingles race across my skin, down my throat, tightening my nipples.

His eyes find mine, and I hope mine don't give away how much the small contact has affected me.

He smears a bit of the greasepaint onto my cheek, his thumb easing over my skin, then takes one of my hands in his, and smooths a streak of grease onto my palm. Oh God. There are a lot of nerve endings there, and he has turned them all on.

He rubs his thumb slowly, languidly over the end of the grease stick, his gaze holding mine like a challenge, and my knees get watery.

And then—his eyes still dark and unrelenting on my face—his thumb moves across the top of my breast, over the plumped-up curve, brushing fire there, while his pupils flare dark with approval.

14

SHANE

I wasn't kidding about the sexy-mechanic kink. And that was before I stroked greasepaint onto her breast.

Now I know exactly how her skin feels—lush and satiny. Only the fact that I'm in a room full of other people —including her sister—keeps me from opening my hand over that curve, cupping her, pushing that ridiculous bra thing down, finding her nipple, and rolling it between my thumb and forefinger.

She pulls back, turns away, and disappointment and relief flood me at the same time.

Sonya is staring at us, her mouth slightly open.

"Ah," she says. "Um."

"What?" I demand.

"I just—I—never mind."

"You know what?" I say. "If you need to get back to work, I think we'll just set up a tripod to film the proposal." I'd originally asked Nia if she'd be our videographer, but for some reason, that idea no longer appeals to me.

"I think that's an excellent idea," Nia says. "It might be

better if you had some…"

She trails off.

"Privacy," Sonya finishes for her.

"Yes. Privacy. I'd better get back to the theater."

"And I need to get back to Hott Spot," Bella says.

"All of us," Reggie chimes in.

The women gather up their things and stuff them back into shopping bags and totes, heading out the door. Sonya and Reggie are the last to leave.

Sonya takes Ivy's hand. "Hey. If you need someone to go wedding-dress shopping with you, call me, okay?"

Ivy's expression softens. "Okay," she says.

"I'm in, too," Reggie says.

Sonya rolls her eyes in her friend's direction. "Just know that if you let her come along? We're totally going to end up thrifting for your dress."

"She doesn't lie," Reggie admits. "But I'm a fucking genius at it."

Ivy laughs. "Thanks," she says. "I haven't really plugged in here—I was…gun-shy after LA."

"Yeah, I bet it's tough to know who your real friends are there," Sonya says sympathetically.

That's for fucking sure, I think.

Ivy nods, biting her lip.

Someone hurt her, and I'm pretty sure it's Fessa. I want to break his kneecaps.

"Thank you," she says, leaning in and hugging the two women.

They slip out, and we're left alone. It feels like a bad idea. And also the best idea.

"So," Ivy says.

I like the way her gaze keeps slipping away from my face to rake over my torso. I especially like the way it snags at the spot where my breeches ride low on my hips. "So," I echo.

"Where are we doing this proposal?"

"The engine bay of the *Atticus*?"

She grins. "Lashed to a spire?"

"We're going to have to settle for something a little more down-to-earth."

"My backyard?"

"Sounds good."

I gather the tripod and phone adapter, and we walk through Ivy's tidy kitchen and into her backyard.

"This is—beautiful."

It's a garden, like the front yard, but whereas the front has a wild country-garden feel, this is sculpted and tamed and curated. There's a small patio with a rattan sofa, two chairs, and a glass coffee table. Blooms burst from pots and from beds that surround the patio, in small clusters of colors and shapes.

"Thanks," she says, blushing. She has tiny freckles on her nose and across her cheeks, amping up her girl-next-door appeal. "This house was my gift to myself when I left LA. I used up the last of my *Bridge* earnings for safety, security, and a place to call home."

Her eyes move over the fruits of her labor, and I watch the small, self-satisfied smile that blossoms. She's the prettiest thing in this gorgeous landscape.

"What if you sit in that chair—" I point. "I'll set this up here..."

She nods, and I set up the phone where I indicated. She

takes a seat on the couch.

"Maybe you're sitting out here, reading, and I surprise you?"

She dashes inside and comes back out with a book. *Marriage of Inconvenience* by Penny Reid. Seems...apt.

She curls up with her book in the corner of the chair. "How do we explain the fact that I have greasepaint on my face?"

I shrug. "You were fixing the car and then took a break in the shade."

She shakes her head, rolling her eyes.

"Your fans are not going to ask questions. They're just going to love this."

"Except for the disappointed suitors."

"Screw them," I say. "I revel in their disappointment."

Truer words were never spoken. Anyone who doesn't want to know who Ivy is beyond the character on the screen is missing out and doesn't deserve her.

"One more thing," I say.

"What's that?"

"Wait here."

I go back to my car and grab what I need from the back seat. When I step out into the backyard again, her eyes get big.

"Is that a real sword?"

"It's a stunt sword. Aluminum. They use steel for up-close shots and this for wider shots."

"Huh."

"Women love swords."

She rolls her eyes again.

"Tell me you don't."

She bites her lip. "I—damn it. It's pretty hot," she admits.

I sheath it while she watches. Very slowly and deliberately.

"Seriously?" she demands.

I grin and shrug. "Whatever the audience wants."

I start recording. She tucks herself back into the corner with her book. I stride into the frame. She does an admirable job of pretending I've startled her.

I try to kneel, and my sword jams itself into a space between the patio stones and I almost fall over.

Ivy dissolves in giggles. "Lord Extyllior," she says when she can speak again. "I think your sword is too big."

"No such thing as a sword that's too big." I work the tip of the sword free from where it's wedged. "Just a guy who hasn't taken his time the way he should."

Her eyes widen and her lower lip softens. And I notice. I notice all the fuck over.

I'm not that interested in proposing marriage right now. What I really want to do is slide that other overall strap off her shoulder, lick the satiny skin I touched earlier, and...

And what? Ivy has done nothing to indicate she'd be up for something casual—if anything, she's given every indication that she's the small-town, settle-down type.

Rein it in, Shane.

"Let's take that from the top."

I start over again, this time swinging the sword out behind me before I kneel.

Her eyes do another perusal of my torso, and her tongue peeks out—just the tip, so small and quick I doubt the camera even caught it. Though I hope it did. Not that

I'm planning to watch the unedited video a time or two or ten thousand tonight. And the earlier one, too—the one where her eyes tell me she likes the idea of me taking my time with her and her lower lip invites me in.

Focus, Shane.

I sweep my hand in front of her, revealing a small black velvet box, open.

And now her eyes come up to my face, and I can see it: genuine surprise. And I feel an echo in my own chest—my pleasure at hers.

The stones form a flower, a round-cut center yellow diamond surrounded by smaller white diamond drops—petals.

I figured she has to wear this damn fake ring for months. She shouldn't hate it. And what better ring for a gardener than a flower?

"Oh my God, Shane, it's *gorgeous*," she says, pressing her hand to her lush mouth.

I try to ignore how much I like her surprise and delight. I try not to think of other ways I could surprise and delight her, other things I could do that would make her touch her mouth like that.

I try not to think of my fingers on her lips.

Or what else I could press to that soft pinkness, urging her to open for me...

I'm glad I'm kneeling, that I'm angled slightly away from the camera and that viewers' attention will be on Ivy's captivated—captivating—face and not on what's happening in my breeches.

Pull it together, man. Focus.

"Ivy. Will you do me the honor of marrying me?"

15

SHANE

A couple of days later, I video call my dad from my hotel room.

When I went to LA at eighteen, I had this fantasy that my dad and I would be buds. That we'd go to Lakers and Dodgers games and "grab lunch"—that kind of thing.

In practice, our paths only cross when he wants to talk business, so normally I wouldn't call to update him about a life thing—like getting engaged—but in this case, since there are publicity implications and he hates to be blind-sided, I loop him in.

"Shane!" he says.

"Hi, Dad. I'm getting married."

My dad's response is a big, scoffing laugh.

"No, I'm serious. The proposal's gonna be on TikTok and Insta later today." My publicist worked her magic, editing the video to perfection, and I'll give her the heads-up to post it as soon as I get off this call.

"Oh, *that* kind of getting married," my dad says. "With the big honking finger quotes around it."

I inherited my nonstick surface from my dad. Long before I moved back to LA, my mom and granddad used to tell me that I reminded them of him. Even as a little kid, I was pretty sure it wasn't meant to be a compliment...but I tried to take it as one. My dad might not have been the best husband or the best dad, but he was a successful actor, director, and producer—all things I wanted to be when I "grew up."

I followed in his footsteps. I was a theater kid who also lettered in baseball and basketball, and I swashbuckled my way through my teen years. I lost my virginity at age sixteen to an older girl. I was a fun project for her, and she was a good time for me, and it worked out perfectly.

I had a hell of a good time in high school, and it didn't really occur to me at first that it was strange that I was always the one who broke it off. That I never wanted to reciprocate an *I love you*. It didn't really penetrate my brain that I was unusual until I got to LA and women started asking me if I'd been in love before—which was often a prelude to them telling me they were falling for me. And they were shocked when I said no.

I'd been in LA just a year when I met April. We were filming a commercial together, and we were at the exact same hungry, ambitious moment in our careers. We hit it off, decided to become roommates, and then became really good friends—the kind who stay up all night talking, grab breakfast in an all-night diner, and have each other's backs through all the miseries of trying to climb the Hollywood ladder.

April was the best friend I'd ever had, but she wanted us to be more than friends. I cared enough about her—for the first time ever—to take a shot at it. But no matter how hard I tried, I couldn't feel what she wanted—needed—me to feel.

After things between me and April crashed and burned, I confided what had happened to my dad—one of the few times I opened up to him. He shrugged and said it was good for me to realize that Hadley men don't fall in love.

He said the biggest favor I could do myself and the women in my life was to let them know that up front.

I've tried to do that ever since.

"Of course," I tell my dad. "The finger-quotes kind of wedding."

"Well, congrats," he says offhandedly.

It's not like I expected champagne and confetti, of course, but for some inexplicable reason I feel let down.

I run a hand through my hair. I haven't slept great the last few nights, since we made the video. I've been mentally planning for our first meeting with Hanna and Weggers, coming up this Friday. But that's only half of what's kept me up. I also can't get Ivy out of my head. That dangling overall strap, the other one still clinging to her bare shoulder, the skimpy top underneath, that wrinkly fabric that hid what her nipples might have done when I brushed greasepaint over the curve of her tits. Leaving it to my imagination.

Then the sword jokes, the widening of her eyes, the softening of her mouth, the hardening of my cock.

I'm hard every time I think about it again, lying in bed, trying to respectfully not jerk off to a fantasy of stripping off those overalls and discovering her panty-less and wet for me...

And failing.

It's a wonder I don't have calluses.

"I wish you'd brought me into this," my dad says. "We could have strategized it together. There are a lot of alliances I would have liked to make. Who is she? I hope you picked well."

I picked well.

"It's Eva Scott. Of *Bridge*."

My dad hums. "I'm looking her up," he says. "Oh. Interesting. She left acting and now she does community theater and summer programs for teens. Yes. I like her for you. Brilliant choice for image cleanup. People will know who she is, but she's God's gift to *wholesome*. And she doesn't have a big fan base that'll go after you when you two get divorced."

My dad's like this: pragmatic and no-nonsense, but for some reason this rubs me the wrong way.

"She's bigger than you think, Dad. She has a cult following. The show's popular on Screenflix."

"'Popular on Screenflix,'" my dad says scornfully. "A dying platform. Look, she's definitely not my first choice, but she'll do."

"She's my first choice."

My voice is tighter and harder than I intended.

"Enough of that." My dad makes a dismissive gesture. "I've got to get to another meeting in fifteen. Let's talk about this *Life of Thor* movie. The more I hear, the more I like it for you. It'll capture mainstream audience that's hooked on the Marvel Thor, plus appeal to the"—he tips his nose up with his finger to indicate snobbery—"one percent. And that means good box office and good reviews." He rubs his fingers together, indicating cash. Which is both par for the course with him and also kind of a joke because I think my dad has enough money at this point that he could burn it for fuel in his marble fireplace.

"Plus I've been wanting to get you an in with John Allison for a long fucking time."

The thing about my dad is that he really *has* had my back. Ever since I showed up on his doorstep, he's been looking out for ways to get me more and more success. He's got a talent for predicting how well projects will fly. So if I was a little disappointed at eighteen that he didn't want to father-and-son-it-up on the town, I got over it.

"I've also been looking at Tim Ernst's indie project," I tell him. "It's not a huge money maker, but it's a good David and Goliath story, and I think it needs to be told. The water supply is a real issue, and it's shittiest for poor people."

My dad rolls his eyes. "If I had a dollar for every David and Goliath feel-good, *this is gonna change the world* story that bombed at the box office—"

You could burn them in your marble fireplace.

Usually my dad's bottom-line obsession doesn't get to me, but today it's pissing me off.

I used to love acting, but Hollywood has wrung a lot of the joy out of it lately. I feel like I'm going through the motions, like the pageantry of being famous is more important than what I'm doing on-screen. I've been thinking lately that if I could just find a project I was passionate about, maybe I could turn that around.

"Look," my dad says, "go ahead and talk to Ernst if you feel like you have to play out that option, but keep your eye on the ball here. *Thor*. John Allison. Box office and reviews. I'm gonna set up a meeting with John for the end of this week. Can you fly down?"

I open my mouth to protest, to argue for pursuing the Tim Ernst indie, but then I close it. Whatever else you can say about my dad, his instincts are dead on. Before I stomp my feet and throw a tantrum, I should check out both options.

My dad may be a bit of a *cash is king* guy, but I gotta be fair—his advice has never led me astray.

Everything else up to this point has been a dress rehearsal.

This is the real thing.

I've never been one to get stage fright, but I have it today.

Shane and I are meeting with Hanna to nail down wedding details. And Arthur Weggers, the one man we have to actually convince that our marriage is real, will be there.

Shane picks me up at my house. I'm ready to run out to meet him, but he parks the car and ambles up my front walk. He gives good swagger, and this time he looks like he stole his clothes from cowboy central casting: green plaid shirt, Wranglers, a thick-buckled belt, boots, and a cream-colored cowboy hat.

On the other hand, maybe it's not all an act. He did grow up on a ranch. Maybe he's returning to his roots.

I have so many questions, but in the short term, I'll just enjoy the view.

As he gets closer, I can see that he's frowning. There's a small crease between his brows. He hasn't shaved; there's a rough shadow on his jaw. I wonder what it would feel like under my palm.

"You look like I feel," I tell him.

The corner of his mouth turns up. "Slept like shit," he admits. "Woke up to my socials going nuts."

"Mine, too. Thousands of new follows. Loads of DMs. Luckily, so far at least, not too much ugliness. A little bit of, 'Ugh, she's let herself go so much since *Bridge*,' but whatever—I can take it."

His eyes travel over me from head to toe. "You don't look like you've let yourself go one bit," he says. It's almost a drawl, and it curls, warm and molasses, in my belly.

"You just can't help yourself, can you?" I tease. "Can't turn off the flirt?"

"Not with you," he says easily.

I look around, but there's no one. No neighbors watching us, no paparazzi lurking—at least not that I can see. "There's no one here. You can let down the act."

"Not an act." He shrugs.

I don't know what to say to that.

He raises an eyebrow. "You want my assistant to handle your social media explosion?"

It's tempting. "No—I dropped a line to my old assistant to see if she wants a short-term gig handling my social media till this all dies down. Luckily, we're still on good terms, she needs work, and the answer was yes."

"Let me pay for it at least. Since all this"—he gestures—"is my fault."

I tilt my head. "I need this, too, remember?"

"Still," he says. "Lord Extyllior can foot the bill for that bullshit."

"I'll think about it," I say, and he nods.

"And if you end up needing security—"

"Security?" I yelp.

"The paparazzi are going to swarm your house sometime in the next twenty-four hours. The question is just how fast they lose interest and move on."

Panic tingles in my chest.

He must see it because he says, "It'll be okay. I promise. Just let me handle the security side."

I'm too much of a control freak to be reassured by that, but I let it go—for now. We have enough other stuff to think about at the moment. "How are you feeling about this Hanna-and-Weggers gig?"

"I'm a wreck," he admits "I don't know how this goes down. My sister can't lie to save her life. I really don't want to be the Hott brother who fucks it all up."

On impulse, I reach out and touch his arm. "We've got this," I say. "You're Shane Fucking Hott. You own the skies. You're a kickass actor. Surely you can fool one asshole lawyer."

He draws himself up to his—impressive—full height. "You think I'm a kickass actor?"

"I think it takes a lot of range to play Lord Extyllior *and* Casey Riggs."

"You watched *Intention*?"

I nod. "Last night."

He perks up a bit. "And you liked it?"

"Loved it."

It's a sci-fi rom-com, and his character is the nerdy sidekick friend, all comic relief and physical humor, with an adorable come-from-behind side-plot romance. It's just about the polar opposite of Lord Extyllior, and Shane is hilarious and lovable.

"You were great as Casey."

"I want to do another indie flick," he says suddenly.

"Yeah? You should."

"You think?"

"I think you can do anything you want. You steal the spotlight every time you're on-screen. And you were brilliant as Casey."

For the first time in our acquaintance, Shane blushes. And I realize that for all his bravado—and Oscar nods—he, too, sometimes needs reassurance from the people he respects.

The part I wasn't expecting was that "people he respects" apparently includes me.

I bite back a smile.

"You enjoying the ring?" he asks, gesturing at my hand.

I roll my hand back and forth, admiring the sunlight sparkling off the flower. I'm more touched than I want to admit that he chose something I love so much. In all the time I was with Anthony, he never bought me something I adored like this.

"It's beautiful," I say. "I can't stop looking at it. I'm going to miss it when I have to give it back."

"You don't have to give it back. It's a gift."

"Uh, *no*," I say. "That's not happening. But thank you." A thought strikes me. "You know what part of our story we never got straight?"

"What?" he asks.

"You told everyone we had a private proposal before our fake proposal. What was it?"

He grins. "Didn't get that far. We'll have to make it up. What would you *want* it to be?"

"Not a marching band."

"Yeah, I figured."

"No costumes."

He tilts his head. "Okay. That's a lot of things you don't want. But what about what you *would* want? Candlelight? Roses? Being flown to Paris?"

I shake my head. "I don't think so. I'm not really a pomp-and-circumstance gal. I wouldn't have wanted it to be anything planned or fancy. Just—you know, honest. Down-to-earth."

He's quiet before he says, "Yeah, that fits. We know it's right between us, and it's the one thing in our lives that doesn't have to be a performance. So more like at home, in a quiet room, me on one knee?"

I nod, trying not to be unsettled by the wistfulness in his words—*we know it's right between us*—or the image of him on one knee *at home* and how tempting I find both.

And maybe he senses my unease because his grin slips. He reaches out, pushing a lock of my hair behind my ear. "Ivy," he says, his eyes dark on mine. "I just want to say— whatever happens in there, I really appreciate you doing this."

His fingers have left a line of heat across my cheek, my temple, my scalp. I swallow, hard, and look away, trying to get my feet back under me.

That's when I see it. A parked car on the street, with a man inside. Window down. Phone up.

Our first paparazzo.

I let out a breath I hadn't known I was holding. Everything suddenly makes way more sense—the flirting, the earnest moment, the touching, the heat in his eyes. He's putting on a show.

I swallow an unexpected surge of disappointment and steel myself for the next act. "Let's go get ourselves an Academy Award for Best Bullshit Wedding."

17

IVY

"Let me just lay this on the table up front," says the little bald-headed grumpy attorney. "I don't buy it."

My heart thumps against my ribs.

It shouldn't surprise me that Weggers doesn't believe us, and it shouldn't surprise me that he's being confrontational. Shane warned me it would probably go down like this.

I don't think he's exactly an evil guy, he told me, brow furrowed. *It's more like he promised my granddad he'd see this through and he can't let it go.*

That much is clear as Weggers eyes us suspiciously.

I could let Shane handle this. It's not my family's will. Technically, this isn't my situation to save. But then I think about the lengths Shane went to earlier this week to get me the killer wedding proposal I needed. And how he said he'd handle the security stuff.

For better or for worse, it seems like we're in this together.

I'm used to having my sister on my side—but it's been a long time since I felt like I had a partner in crime.

The realization sends a wash of warmth through me, and I lean in, giving Arthur Weggers my best shy smile. "I know it seems like this is out of the blue. But Shane and I had mad chemistry from the start. I just didn't think he was the kind of guy who *could* settle down. But when I ran into him in Rush Creek this time, I saw a different side of him."

Weggers flinches. He's surprised I jumped in. He was expecting Shane to do all the talking.

"If we could get on with the meeting?" Hanna inserts before Weggers can regroup for another assault.

Her timing and tone are perfect. I have no idea why Shane was worried about her. She sounds vaguely irritated and impatient, fiddling with a pen as she swings her gaze from one of us to the next.

No one dares to obstruct her. We all just *nod*.

Shane looks utterly unconcerned—or he's feigning it well. He's sitting back in his chair, posture relaxed, legs slung out in front of him, every inch the cowboy taking an afternoon nap on a hay bale. All long, lean muscle on display, making my mouth water. He just needs to cover his face with his hat to block out the sun.

If I didn't know he hadn't slept last night, I'd think nothing about this situation was worrying him in the slightest.

"Let's start with the legalities," Hanna says. "I'm going to have you fill out the marriage license online—I do this because you wouldn't believe the number of people who forget to file their marriage licenses—and then you'll have to go pick it up and pay for it at the clerk's office."

Shane fills out the online form while I stand behind him. The moment calls for something, so I rest a hand on his back. Weggers scowls.

Okay, maybe the hand is a mistake. The long lean muscles in Shane's back bunch as he shifts in his seat, and heat radiates into my fingers. My whole body attunes itself to his, warming and melting. It's unbelievably distracting. I keep thinking about what I want to do with my hand— slide it up to his shoulder, down his arm. Best case, he would turn his chair around so I could palm the ridged abs I saw when he was outfitted as Lord Extyllior. And then I would slide my palm down and feel the heft of that thick belt buckle against my palm.

Right before I worked it free and wrapped my hand around him.

There is nothing fake about how much I want to touch this man everywhere. My fingers curl into the soft fabric of his shirt. He shifts again, pushing his back into my palm, like a cat arching into touch. Or maybe I'm just imagining that. Maybe I just want him to luxuriate in my touch, to crave more of it.

I definitely do.

Because I can, I slide my hand up the groove of his spine and let my palm wander over his shoulder to the thick cap of muscle there. He stiffens under the stroke, and—

I like it so much.

He strikes a key decisively. "There," he says and casually lifts his hand to trap mine. His palm is big and warm, and I want to move exactly never. Maybe he's having the same thought because he leaves his hand there. We're holding hands.

No, I remind myself. We're just playing a part.

I ease my hand out from under his and sink back into my chair.

I can still feel his warmth, even across the small gap between our seats.

Hanna talks us through our intake interview, laying out the choices we still have to make. She suggests a celebrant she likes—a Unitarian minister—and helps us choose a premium e-invitation from a site Hott Springs Eternal partners with.

Weggers pulls out his phone.

"What are you doing?" Shane asks.

"Saving the date," Weggers says. "I wasn't going to go to January and Tobias's wedding, but your grandfather would want me at this one." He glares at us. "Assuming it's real, which he would also want, because you know he had zero patience for fakers and liars."

"You're not invited," Hanna says bluntly.

Shane and I turn to her. She looks *pissed*.

Weggers draws himself up. "I'll be there," he says primly.

I close my eyes. Maybe he'll disappear.

But when I open them again, he's still there, and Hanna has a disgruntled expression that I suspect means she feels like she lost that round. With a sigh, she tells us that normally we'd be way too close to the wedding to risk switching caterers, but in this case, she has an alternative for us.

"My sister-in-law owns Around the Table and does

weddings, and she's killer. The only thing is she doesn't handle the bar, so if you go with her, I have a couple ideas for someone separate to run the bar."

"I've had Around the Table's food before. It's fantastic," I tell Shane.

"Agreed. Amanda's amazing," he says. "And yeah, just bring someone in to do the bar. We don't need personalized signature cocktails or anything."

"Signature cocktails sound fun," I say shyly.

Shane, from the chair next to mine, puts an arm around me. "Then we'll have signature cocktails."

He's laying it on thick, but I decide I'm just going to let myself enjoy it for the moment. If I were getting married, I'd want my future husband to be just like Shane. Smoking hot, physically affectionate, and over-the-top solicitous.

Aside from being fake, he's basically perfect.

"I also suggest you stick with Tobuary's photographer and videographer," Hanna says. "It's too late to swap them out. And their DJ. And ideally their florist?"

"Who's their florist?" I ask.

"I like to work with Big Blooms Floral—any issues with that?"

"I love her work!"

Hanna smiles. "You're into flowers, huh?"

Shane's watching me, his lips curving at the corners. "Have you seen her garden?"

His sister shakes her head.

"It's fucking amazing," he says, smiling at me. I recognize that smile, I realize. It's the one he gave his romantic co-lead in *Intention*. It's Shane's "adoring" smile.

I like it way too much.

Hanna lights up. "We could talk about supplementing with your own flowers. Big Blooms will do that."

"That would be awesome."

Hanna looks back down at her list. "Cake," she says. "You need to stick with Rush Creek Bakery—partly because of the time line and partly because you could not pay me enough to get on Nan's bad side."

I chuckle at that. I know Nan—everyone in town knows Nan, Rush Creek Bakery owner and the town's resident gossip—and I totally sympathize with Hanna's desire not to cross her. "That's fine. Although I'm bummed I don't get to do a cake tasting. To the extent I've ever fantasized about getting married, the two things I was excited about were flowers and cake."

Hanna laughs. "Those are two good things. I can get you a meeting with the florist, definitely, and I'm pretty sure I can get Nan to let you do your own cake tasting, even on our short time line."

"Sweet!" I say. "I have vivid, naughty fantasies involving Better Than Sex cake."

Is it my imagination or does Shane make a choking sound? Is he laughing at me?

Hanna's eyebrows are up as she looks at him.

"That's fine," Shane says, finally recovering his power of speech. "Cake tasting sounds good."

"Two more things." Hanna points at us. "You need to reach out to whoever you want to be in your wedding party and ask them to stand up for you. And you"—she points straight at me this time—"need to find a dress ASAP. I have a couple of people who can do rush alterations, but the dress itself has to be in stock."

"I have a date with Sonya, Reggie, and my sister to do that this weekend," I say.

"Good," she says. "If anyone gives you shit about the short time line, call me. I'll bust some balls."

I snicker at that.

"She's not joking." Shane shakes his head. "I have been on the receiving end of Hanna's anger, and it can definitely impair your ability to have children."

"Also." Hanna lays a hand flat on her desk. "Honeymoon. Get those plans on the books as soon as possible."

"We will," I say, not looking at Shane.

Of course, we're not going to actually book a honeymoon.

Although maybe we have to? To make it look real?

Where would Shane Hott and Eva Scott go on their honeymoon?

To the highest point in the mountaintops?

To the edge of the universe?

I snicker, and Shane shoots me a quizzical look.

Tell you later, I mouth.

When I look back at Hanna, she's watching me curiously.

"And we've set the dates for the bachelor and bachelorette parties," she says.

Wait, what? We don't need those, and Hanna knows it. We're not swearing off sex with other people forever, just for a few months. It would have been easy enough to leave the parties off the list, to just let them go. But maybe Hanna thinks they'll make the fiction more convincing?

She spools off dates and locations for the bachelor and bachelorette parties, which are next weekend. I blink at that. I knew the timeline was short...but everything's happening *fast*.

"Quinn is hosting yours," Hanna tells Shane and then turns to me. "Sonya is hosting yours. And since Sonya says you're going to say you don't know enough people to throw a bachelorette party, she said I have to tell you that she and I have that covered. You just show up. We'll bring the fun."

"Oh," I say. "That's—wow. That's super kind of you."

Hanna shrugs. "You're one of us now," she says.

I know it's for Weggers's benefit, but for a moment, I long for a group of women who actually feel that way about me.

"That's it for today, folks," Hanna says. "I'll have Julia reach out to you to put another meeting on the calendar. And I'll see you back at the ranch."

Weggers rumbles to his feet. "Don't think this is over," he tells Shane.

"I'm not sure what you're talking about," Shane says, "but I know this isn't over. It's the rest of my life." He slips an arm around me and tugs me close.

It feels ridiculously good to be sandwiched between his muscular arm and his hard body, and without quite meaning to, I lean my head on his shoulder and close my eyes.

It's okay to enjoy pretending for just a few minutes, right?

I know what's real, after all.

Still, I open my eyes and look up and find him looking back at me. Maybe he's just acting, but there's so much fondness on his face that I find myself hoping he isn't. That at least he values the time we've spent together so far, the effort we've put in, how good we are when we work together—that he feels like we're friends.

His arm draws tighter around me, and it feels like a yes.

He doesn't release me until he has to let me go so I can climb into the car.

18

SHANE

Ivy says, "I think that went amazingly well!"

"It did." We couldn't have given Weggers a better show. Acting across from Ivy is an absolute joy. I've had lots of leading women...but none I click with as well as Ivy.

Almost too well: When she stroked her hand from my back to my shoulder, my body didn't think we were *just acting*. It was ready to grab that hand and shove it into my pants. Or to pull her down so she was straddling me and kiss the shit out of her.

I did none of that, of course, which is good because leading men who grope their leading women are a) assholes and b) these days—thank God—often out of a job.

"What are we going to do about bridesmaids?" she asks.

"Your sister. Your mom?" I ask.

She shakes her head. "She doesn't know about this. Trying to keep it that way."

"Won't she find out? We're not exactly flying under the radar." No paparazzo yet, to be fair, although as Ivy and I were pulling away from her house earlier, I did think I spotted a lone operator in his ratty car.

"She's in Spain, she's madly in love, and she's news averse, so I have a fighting chance."

"Okay, so who else? You said you don't know a lot of people here. And that you're gun-shy from LA?"

"I lost touch with show friends after I left *Bridge*. It's a long story. Some stuff went down with the crew, and—I needed to start over."

"Any heads I need to knock together?"

She smiles. "No. Just people being people. Believing rumors, taking sides."

I want to know more, but Ivy's already made it clear that stories about the end of her time in LA require alcohol. "What about before that? College?"

"I had good friends in college, but it got weird with them when I got famous. The first time my assistant accidentally replied to one of my personal emails, my friend sent me a ragey response and said she was done. After I did the engine-room scene, one told me that she didn't want anything to do with my kind of 'exposure.' A couple others drifted away."

"Jesus!"

The urge to break a few kneecaps is strong again.

"Obviously they weren't the greatest friends to begin with. It made me realize that you can't trust most people to have your back." She shrugs, trying to make it seem like she doesn't care, but then she bites her lip again.

Maybe I *will* knock a few heads together. How can anyone not want to be Ivy's friend? She's great—smart, funny, kind, gorgeous...though maybe that last one isn't a trait they value? How the hell do I know?

"What about you?"

It takes me a second to realize she's asking about my friends and family. "I have my agent. A few guys I pal around with occasionally. I get friendly with whatever cast and crew I'm filming with. But friends? Not so much."

"Your dad? Are you going to tell him about us?"

Us.

I like the sound of it—more than I should.

Make-believe. That's all this is. Don't read anything into... anything. "He knows."

She raises her eyebrows. "Knows the truth?"

For a moment, I think she's talking about the fact that I've gotten off track a bit. That I've given way too much thought to what it would be like to strip her out of her clothes. Tongue my way down her body. Taste her at great length.

Nope. She means the truth that we're faking it.

Pull it together, Shane.

"Not exactly," I say. "He decided on his own that we're faking it for PR reasons."

"Because he knows you would never *actually* get married?"

"That and because he has a jaded view of relationships. He's not much for connecting with people on anything beyond a transactional level."

I can tell she wants to ask me more, her eyes moving curiously over my face, but she doesn't.

"You have a good relationship with your brothers, though, right?"

"They're good people. But—"

I stop.

"What?" she asks gently.

"We were really close as kids. We had a blood oath that we'd stay in Rush Creek and run the ranch together." I hold up my hand, showing her the scar on the meat of my thumb. "Then we all fucked it up, one by one—me by running away to Hollywood and basically declaring myself in my dad's camp instead of my mom's, granddad's, and theirs. Now we're just a bunch of guys who love Hanna."

Her expression is soft. "I don't know," she says. "Sonya came through for you pretty damn fast when you needed help with the proposal. So I'm guessing that means Quinn loves you a hell of a lot."

Something uncomfortably warm and sloppy rises in my chest. I shrug. "He tolerates me."

"But you will ask your brothers to stand up for you."

"Yeah. I will."

She smiles. "We're lopsided. You have your five sibs, and I just have Nia."

"I've got Easton, too."

"Even worse," she says. "That's six for you."

I'm struck by an idea, but before I can suggest that Sonya and Hanna would be happy to stand up on her side, we turn down her street and I spot the first photographer.

19

SHANE

I yank the wheel and redirect us down a side street.

"Where are you going?"

"Your house is crawling with paparazzi."

"Oh."

"No worries. I'm used to it."

I turn us toward town and the Depot Hotel. The paparazzi situation will probably be even worse there, but I'd rather lure the action toward me than toward Ivy's house.

Sure enough, as we approach the hotel, I can see the small but definitely lively crowd outside. I park down a side street, tucking us into a discreet space for a brief strategy session.

"You trust me?" I ask.

"Haven't we already established that I do?"

"I think last time you told me you didn't. Or at least you couldn't give me a blanket yes."

The dimple deepens in her cheek. "Well. There's been some water under the bridge since then."

I reach between us and grab my phone, banging out a couple of quick texts to Tuck. "I'm texting Tucker," I say. "Because he works in personal security. He stayed in town after Eloise's christening to help Hanna with some heavy lifting. He can break up the crowd at your house and set up a presence there."

She nods. "Thanks."

"How would you feel about vamping for the cameras for a bit? Getting it out of the way? With that and the interviews we have set up for the next few days, we might be able to get them off our backs. It's only news until everyone's had their fill."

She sighs.

"You've got this," I say. "Big smiles, super friendly, zero defensiveness about anything. The next few days'll be hard, and then it'll die down. No one will care by this time next week—take my word for it. People's attention spans are short."

"Until the wedding."

"True. Until the wedding."

She's quiet, and I glance at her. She still looks worried.

"You really hate it, huh? The spotlight?"

"I love the spotlight when I'm performing. And then I just want to be able to get away from it all the rest of the time. But that's not how it works."

"No," I agree, laughing.

"Give me a minute to touch up my makeup?"

I smile. "Of course."

I park within view of the gathered horde, sneaking glances at her as she strokes mascara onto her lashes and smooths a raspberry gloss over her already soft, bright mouth. That mouth. I want things from that mouth.

You told her kissing might be on the table.

Not the kind of kissing you want to do. The kind that goes on for hours. The kind that explores every last inch and curve and fold.

She catches me looking and raises her eyebrows. "Never seen a woman putting makeup on?" she teases.

"Of course I have—I've just never found it so hard to avert my eyes."

She rolls her eyes at me. "Uh-huh."

"It's true," I insist, and she rolls her eyes again.

When she's done, we exit the car and walk up the street arm in arm toward our fan club. No evasive maneuvers, just a slow stroll, drawing a rush of photographers who circle in front of us, calling questions. "Smile," I remind her under my breath, and she does.

I sneak glances because it's that slight secret smile like she knows something about you but isn't telling, and she's aglow. She's the most beautiful woman I've ever seen, and I've seen a lot of beautiful women. I feel a sharp rush of pride in her: this woman is *mine*—

But of course she's *not*.

She's just pretending to be.

I make myself look away, giving the photographers and journalists my best movie-star grin. I consciously tone down the *bad boy* factor. I'm a family man now—or that's what I need them to believe. The more the world believes it, the harder it'll be for Weggers to fight it.

Flashes pop and photographers jockey for space, and

we wait it out patiently, letting them ask us questions, telling the story of how we met. We're both fumbling through the story, but it works perfectly because it means we have to keep turning to each other for confirmation, bouncing our tale back and forth like two people who are so in love they can't remember how they got there. It feels like magic.

It feels like truth.

"Let's see the ring again!"

Ivy holds her hand out for them. The ring looks so good. For a moment I have an impulse: to turn her elegant hands into a garden, flowers on all her fingers.

Silly.

But I can't quite put it out of my head.

"Kiss her!" someone calls.

I don't look at her. I can't.

"Kiss her! Kiss her!"

It's a chant now.

This moment was always going to happen. We both knew it.

"It's okay," she murmurs, and the intimacy of her low, husky voice breaks through my resistance. I bend over and settle my lips on hers. My intention is to linger just long enough for the cameras.

Ivy's eyes drift close, her eyelashes casting shadows on her high cheekbones, and it's that, almost more than the sensation of touching my mouth to hers, that tears the rough sound out of my throat. Too soft, too private for the paparazzo to hear, but I know she hears it because she answers with the grip of her hand on my wrist. Under mine, her lips open, just a fraction. It might be surprise.

Not surprise that I've kissed her—surprise that it's like *this*.

Electric.

I don't know how it happens, but my hands grip her shoulders, one sliding up behind her head, holding her in place so I can take what I crave, which is more of her. Need pins me to the moment and makes me reckless. I forget where we are and who's watching, and my tongue meets hers. For a moment we're slick and greedy together, the sensation rolling straight to my cock.

Her hand on my wrist wraps tighter, like she's determined to hold me there, and her other hand grasps a handful of my shirt.

And then she breaks the kiss.

She smiles shyly in the direction of the paparazzi with their cameras and their shouted questions.

"What's your next project, Shane?"

"Will it be a church wedding?"

"How big will the wedding be?"

"Will April Vahl be invited?"

I scowl, still off-balance from the way Ivy's mouth hijacked my brain. "You got what you came for," I say. "Now get out of here."

Eventually the cluster breaks up, and it's just us standing in front of my hotel.

"So," she says.

"So," I say.

"That was great!" she says, and I almost say, *God, yes, that was hot as fuck*, but before I can get the words out, she adds, "You're a good co-lead. I think we were really convincing."

Convincing.

She means the kiss.

Our acting.

Right. We just pulled off one of the more difficult parts of this act—convincing the public that we're for real. No doubt left in anyone's mind after that kiss.

"Oh, yeah. Definitely," I say.

But oh God.

I want to kiss her again.

Which is absolutely, positively not going to happen. The last thing this situation needs is blurry lines and the potential for someone to get hurt or confused about the rules.

The last thing this situation needs is my hands all over her perfect ass and my cock rubbing against the V of her jeans and my mouth teasing her lips, jaw, throat, earlobes.

I'm hard again.

I grab for my phone, check in with my brother's messages.

"I'll take you home now," I say. "Tuck's there."

She smiles. "That was fast. Sounds like a guy who loves you."

"Or one who just wants Hanna to keep her business as much as I do."

"Or both," she says with a small shrug.

"He says he sent everyone who was there over here. He called a friend of his who lives in Bend and also works private security. She'll cover you till this dies down if you want."

"I don't have the money for that kind of—"

I wave her off. "It's on me. I set this in motion. The least I can do is make sure someone has an eye on you."

She looks uncertain again, and for the first time since Arthur Weggers made me read that goddamned letter aloud, I wonder if I'm doing the right thing. If you'd asked me that day if anything mattered besides making sure that Hanna kept her business, I would have said no. But right now, the idea of causing Ivy pain or discomfort, of forcing her into this spotlight she really doesn't want feels all wrong.

"You don't have to do this."

The words come out in a rush. I have no right to say it to her because Hanna should be my first priority. My only priority. But I'm not thinking right now. I'm just trying to put a smile back on Ivy's face.

She looks away, her eyes sweeping over the facade of the Western-style hotel, up the main street.

Then she looks back, biting her lower lip. The lower lip that a moment ago was soft as silk under my tongue.

"Nah," she says. "I figure the only way out at this point is forward." She waves a hand.

"You sure?"

"Yup."

And thank *fuck* because I almost lost control of the situation right there. I almost let that kiss scramble my brains and make me think that—

I'm not even sure what. But it almost made me throw away something that isn't mine to throw away.

I need to get a grip.

"We should probably..." I gesture in the direction of the car, and she makes a sound of assent.

We head back there, and it isn't until after I've dropped her off, my lips still tingling and my cock still heavy, that I wonder how I'm going to survive this thing I've done to myself.

20

SHANE

"So how long are you back for?" my dad asks over a business lunch at Deliciosa. The restaurant is all windows and white walls, red leatherette chairs, and white café tables.

"Just long enough to take care of some odds and ends."

I came to LA to do business, but if I'm being completely honest with myself, I was glad to get the hell out of Rush Creek. I needed to catch my breath and figure some things out.

Some things like, *What the fuck was that kiss? And when can I do that again?*

Except that's not the way this is supposed to go.

I more or less promised Ivy that there would be no shenanigans.

The answer to *When can I do that again?* is *Never*.

So I ran like hell away from temptation and threw myself into work.

But it's tough to get away from Ivy. Like right now I'm

eating a Buddha bowl and drinking a green smoothie and thinking about her Hollywood-food snark. She isn't wrong.

"Rumor has it John Allison *loves* you for the role."

There's no rumor involved here. My dad got on the horn with Allison three seconds after I walked out of his office, and both of us know it.

Today was the meeting my dad set up with Allison and the meeting I set up with Tim Ernst. And things pretty much turned out the way I thought they would. I loved Ernst's vision, and he and I hit it off.

I liked Allison, too—neither of us made it as far as we've come by being hard to get along with—but I just didn't feel the same connection to either the man or the movie as I did with Ernst and his project.

"Yeah. Allison seemed enthusiastic."

I'm pretty sure my own lack of enthusiasm is obvious in my voice, but my dad's too buoyant to catch it. "He adores your work," he says. "He's ready to go ahead with you. Shane, this is huge."

"I'm not sure I'm going to take *Thor*," I say. "I also met with Tim Ernst."

"Good, good," my dad says, almost absent-mindedly. He has his phone out and is tapping out a message to someone. "I know you felt like you needed to check that out."

Irritation rises in me. He's making it sound like Ernst is a just a box I need to tick before I agree to be Thor. "It's not just due diligence. I like the project. So I have to give it some thought. I'm not ready to commit to Allison."

My dad leans in. He puts a hand on my arm. Warm. Paternal. "Tim's film isn't the right choice for you. It's not commercial enough. It won't kill it at the box office like *Life of Thor* will. You have to look at the whole context of your career."

My dad says things like that a lot...but in this case, I realize that he actually means the whole context of the career *he wants for me.*

Which isn't necessarily the career *I* want for me.

I've never had to tell my dad no about a job. It just hasn't come down to that. We've always wanted the same thing.

But that's because up till this point, he's been pulling strings to get me to the top of the heap. Now I'm at the top... and I don't need his help.

I guess that means we won't have a lot more to do with each other going forward, since our interactions are so focused on my work. Theoretically, that shouldn't make me sad—there's nothing to lose since there's not much between us besides business—but I still feel a pang.

That said, I can't walk away from what I know is right for me. I think of Ivy saying *I think you can do anything you want* after I told her I want to do an indie flick.

I liked it. I liked it a fucking lot. I want to justify her faith in me.

"Ernst's film does have commercial potential. Maybe not as much as Allison's, but I don't need a lot of money. I can afford to take something that has meaning for me."

My dad frowns. "You've worked really hard to get to the top," he says. "I don't want to see you throw that away on some indie project."

"That's not how I see it," I say. "I see it as I'm at the top of the heap, I earned the money I always only dreamed of —and now I get to make some real choices. And if it's a choice between a box-office smash that doesn't have a lot of soul or something that really speaks to me, that's what I'm going to do."

"Just don't do anything hasty," my dad says.

"I won't," I say. "I'll think about it."

He gets up. "Lunch is on me. Text me the total, and I'll Venmo you. Think about *Thor*," he says, patting me on the shoulder, and I watch his back recede through the crowd in the restaurant.

I should feel a sense of freedom—I held my ground, I made my point—but it doesn't quite feel like a win.

I guess in a lot of ways, I'm still that eighteen-year-old boy who wanted a dad and ended up with a manager.

21

IVY

"**N**o."

The flat rejection comes from Nia, who runs her critical eye over my whole body and dismisses the dress summarily.

Which is fine because I *hate* it. It's like an entire tulle factory ate too many glitter cupcakes and threw up.

"Yeah, no," Sonya says.

I look to Hanna and Reggie.

Reggie shrugs one shoulder, as if to say, *I can't help you if you decide that overgrown marshmallow puff is a dress.*

Hanna frowns. She told me she's mostly here to flex her muscle with the bridal shops and make sure they give me a good deal. "I don't know," she says. "You're talking to a woman who wore a plain, purple ModCloth dress—with pockets!—to her own wedding." She tilts her head, a small smile creeping over her face. "I will say the expression on Easton's face when I came down the aisle was kind of worth it. Also, Easton in a tux pretty much killed the few remaining brain cells I still had. That man."

She sighs happily, and I feel a pang of longing because she's so obviously gone for her husband.

"You guys still going out tonight?" Sonya asks.

"Yeah," Hanna says. "Trying out that new sitter. Do you know how long it's been since the two of us went anywhere together, alone? You'd think with all the potential grandmas and aunties I'd be rolling in babysitters, but lately you have to practically get on a waiting list to get grandma time, and the aunties are all mommies, and—I'm so, so excited just to sit and stare at him across a table."

Aw. That's so stinkin' cute.

And instead of getting closer to finding something like that for myself, I've gotten into this tangle with Shane.

Shane, who left for LA the morning after I lost my mind and tried to lick his mouth.

That kiss.

My face gets hot with shame thinking about it. That was the least professional moment in my entire on-screen career. I grabbed his wrist. I *moaned*, for fuck's sake. And I totally, completely stuck my tongue into his mouth.

And then I remembered who and where I was—and why—and managed to save the moment from disaster.

I think I was actually pretty calm and cool about it, given that my heart was pounding and my core was throbbing and every cell in my body was begging for another chance at Shane Hott's mouth.

Then he went to LA, which was actually great because it sent my brain a nice, clear message—he isn't interested in more kissing.

Signed, sealed, delivered.

Now I peel myself out of the tulle vomit. "We've been at

this for *hours*. And I still haven't seen anything I can imagine myself actually wearing, let alone allowing myself to be photographed in and posted to social media and—"

I try not to think too hard about the wedding day itself because the idea of that much attention being paid to me makes me feel like *I* ate too many glitter cupcakes.

"I have an idea," Reggie says

We all turn to her.

"I think we should go thrifting."

Hanna mutters, "Big surprise."

Reggie's way of dressing is…distinctive. Short skirts, goth-style makeup, multicolored hair. Today she's also wearing lace stockings and a black lace top and rubber-duck earrings. I'm a little wary of taking fashion advice from her but also curious. And it's not like we've found anything good here. Plus I'm grateful for the subject change. I don't really want to get into a mental excavation of that kiss.

I can save that for when I'm alone in bed.

Sonya looks at Hanna. Hanna looks at Nia. Nia looks at me and shrugs. "Not the worst idea I've heard today," she says.

Which is how we find ourselves in a huge consignment shop in Bend, the biggest "city" close to Rush Creek.

We cluster into the no-nonsense dressing room with several *I don't hate this, but it doesn't really fit* white dresses.

"This bodice fits perfectly—"

"But there's a huge stain on the skirt," Hanna says with a sigh.

"And I love this skirt, but you could fit several of me into the top. And it's too long."

"So what you're saying," Sonya says, "is that if someone had the sewing skills to attach this bodice to this skirt, but hemmed to your height, you'd have the perfect wedding gown?"

We all turn to look at her.

"Look." She crosses her arms. "I'm not a professional seamstress or a dressmaker. But I'm good with a machine and I've done garment construction, and I'm totally willing to give it a shot. If you trust me."

I've been asked to trust a lot of people recently, and Sonya's definitely not the worst of them. I shrug. "Sure. Go for it."

After all, it's not like I'm *really* getting married. It's not like I'll be showing photos of myself in this dress to my grandkids someday, beaming at them as I say, *I remember the first time I ever saw your granddad.*

Although I do. I remember the way his eye caught mine in the Hott Spot hallway. I remember thinking, *OMG that guy is hot.* And I remember my body going unexpectedly, instantly molten.

"Ive?" Nia says. "You with us?"

"Uh, yeah," I say.

"Penny for your thoughts."

"I was just thinking we should have videoed more of this," I lie.

"It's not too late!" my sister crows, pulling her phone out.

"That dueting thing you and Shane are doing is *adorable,*" Sonya says.

"Thanks."

Shane's assistant, who is a social media genius, decided

that while we were apart he would have Shane duet videos of me as the two of us separately go about our wedding planning and caption them with lines from Shane about how much he misses me and wishes he could be with me. They've been wildly popular. There's one of Hanna and me working with the florist on arrangement ideas while Shane does a video call with the photographer, another one of me working on evites alongside Shane replying to RSVPs, and a bunch more.

"Let's get you into and out of a couple of these dresses again," Nia says. "Ones you're not going to actually wear, or it'll ruin the wedding-day surprise. And then Shane can put on and take off his tux in the duet. That'll be a big hit." She smirks.

I'm not sure I can survive that video, but I don't say that out loud. Of course, everyone in this dressing room knows I kissed Shane—because that video was all over the internet for days—but no one knows how much I liked it. Or that I've been trying to restrain myself from Googling *Shane Hott in a tux* so I can brace myself for our wedding day.

"No. Nope," Hanna says. "My brother. Nope. No undressing videos." She points a finger at Reggie. "And if such a thing ever happens, no one is—under any circumstances—to share the video with me. Do you understand how traumatic that would be?"

"Cross my heart and hope to die." Reggie completes the gesture with a dagger to the chest. She turns to me. "I can't believe you've had sex with Mavryx."

"With Shane," I automatically correct, then blush ferociously because, of course, *I haven't*. Not that they know that. Well, Sonya, Nia, and Hanna probably do. But now I can't correct the record in either direction because…

Well, fuck.

"I won't ask if it's like the movies," Reggie teases.

"I've only seen the first one," I confess.

I say it because if I don't say that, I might say, *I don't know; I haven't* had *sex with him*, and that will open Pandora's box. But as soon as the words are out of my mouth, they all turn on me in one coordinated movement, mouths gaping.

"Wow," Reggie says. "That's…willpower."

"It's more like living under a rock," I admit.

"I don't think I'd want to watch my fiancé have sex in a movie," Sonya asks. "You might be better off not watching."

I bite my lip. Technically, of course, he's not my fiancé. *And* my curiosity has been growing with every mention of this movie, *especially* since that kiss.

Maybe getting to watch Shane—ack, Mavryx—have sex would take the edge off my craving for actual sex with him?

"Don't watch," Nia says, her expression concerned— because she's my sister, and she probably tracked almost my whole train of thought. "Sonya's right."

"I won't."

My words lack conviction. I can feel myself waffling.

"He's been gone a while," Reggie says. "You must miss him."

I love the fact that the woman who wears all black is this group's hopeless romantic. "Yeah," I tell her.

Then I freeze, the stained skirt held between my hands.

Because it's *true*.

I *miss* him.

When I look up, they're all watching me, but it's Sonya's eyes that catch and hold mine. No irony there, no tease. Just a soft sympathy.

"The Hott brothers," she says, smiling. "No mere mortal woman stands a chance." And touches my shoulder, a gesture of solidarity.

God, I think. *I hope you're wrong.*

22

IVY

You know how sometimes you torture yourself even though you know it's a terrible idea?

The house is empty. The security guard who Tuck found for me is gone now that the initial buzz about the wedding has died down a bit and Shane's assistant and publicist have taken control of the messaging. My security detail will rejoin me closer to the wedding and be at my side through all the pre-wedding festivities, but for now, it's just me.

I saunter into the living room like it's nothing. Like I'm not about to do what I'm about to do. This makes zero sense because there's nobody to pretend for, but...

Well, all the world's a stage, and I'm my own best audience.

I turn on my TV setup. I flip through my choices—I could rewatch *Crash Landing on You* (one of my comfort binges) or I could start *Queen Charlotte*...

Still pretending I'm not doing this.

Or I could watch the second *Crown of Spires* movie. *Dark Skies*. The one with the infamous spire sex scene.

It's a terrible idea. What good could possibly come of it?

I hover my finger over the remote button.

You know how this ends.

I cue it up.

And *wow*.

All things being equal, I probably wouldn't be the biggest fan of the *Crown of Spires* series. I don't usually love fantasy. But this is a terrific story. The redemption arc for Lord Extyllior is killer...and Shane is playing it to the hilt. Wounded hero with a brutal past, trying his best to be a good person for the woman he loves. And it's obvious he loves her with every cell of his very, very hard body (and generous soul).

Lord Extyllior's one of those men who holds himself back, denies himself what he wants...and then falls really fucking hard.

And like a lot of women, I'm a sucker for that kind of man.

By the time their enemies track them down, by the time Lord Extyllior, exhausted near to death from his flight with the woman he won't admit he loves, is forced to stop and find a safe spot to spend the night, I'm all in. Like, *holding my breath, biting my lip, wringing my hands, sweating bullets* all in.

He flies the two of them to the top of the world, to the highest spire in the kingdom. Because that's the only place he knows they're safe, and he will stop at nothing to protect her—even though he won't tell her how he feels about her. (To protect her! *Sigh!*)

His plan is to lash them both to the spire, back to back, so they can get some sleep, regroup, marshal his forces, and fight.

But seeing her like that—bound to the spire, the leather straps he's torn off his own clothes biting into the softness of her skin—snaps the last thread of his self-control. So when she says "Mav—"

It's the first time she's used his first name, Mavryx.

There's pleading in her voice.

He can't resist her, even though he knows he should. She's so *good*, and he's so *bad* for her.

It's because he's such a bad man that he kisses her.

And then—

It's all over. All the self-denial, all the waiting, all the pushing her away. He's kissing her and kissing her, and I have to admit, it's one of the hottest on-screen kisses I've ever seen. Like, *on fire* hot—or maybe that's me, peeling back the blanket I threw over myself and fanning my face as his hands roam her body, wrapping over the leather strap at her wrists.

I'm expecting a fade to black, but I should have known better. This is the famous spire *sex* scene after all, not the famous spire *kiss* scene.

Think *Bridgerton* but hundreds, thousands of feet in the air. Skirts shoved out of the way. Breeches unlaced. Mavryx's back is aglow with effort, bunching and releasing, and that's *before* the camera gives us his gloriously naked ass, demonstrating to the tepid thrusters of this world how it's done. Every last muscle in his body is taut with effort, his hands gripping the spire over their heads, his wings spread, shoulder muscles carved from stone.

Holy. Shit.

And at the same time…

I hate the camera right now.

Because as much as I love all the tanned, ripped *man* on-screen, I'm not seeing what I most want to see. I want the camera on Shane's face. I want to see his eyelids heavy with pleasure, his pupils blown, his lips swollen, mouth open—

"Oh, Christ, I'm sorry—"

Mavryx is on-screen and also in my living room, hands up in the universal symbol of *I'm not going to hurt you.* Not Mavryx. Shane. Shane is in my living room, and it's like coming down from a thousand feet up. Rushing back into my body from a hundred yards away. It's like a collision with the Mack Truck of reality.

He takes a step back, looking like he, too, has been hit with a truck. "Ive, I am *so* sorry— I could hear that you were watching something, and I rang and knocked and texted you, but you didn't hear it—"

He's backing away.

Because I'm sprawled back on the couch, hand tucked between my squeezed-together thighs.

My face flames. I rip my hand away from the soft, hot place between my legs and grab for the remote. But I'm too late.

"Is that…?" Shane has caught sight of the TV. His eyebrows go way up at the sight of himself in his full-on, reverse-side glory.

In an act of absolutely genius tech mastery, I manage to turn off the receiver, TV, and streaming box in rapid succession, and the TV blinks black. For all the good it does me.

He's staring at me.

"Don't," I warn.

"Don't *what*?" he asks.

"Don't lord it over me."

"Ah," he says, and it suddenly occurs to me that he's not smirking. There's no tease in his voice. And his eyes are locked onto my face. My body, which is already hot enough to combust, gets even hotter. He takes a few steps forward and kneels on the floor in front of the couch. "I would never. I mean," he says, his voice low and rough, "I'll leave if you *want* me to leave. But I could also maybe...stay."

"Why would you do that?" I'm torn between embarrassment and curiosity. Desire. Okay, let's call it what it is: *lust*.

He reaches a hand out. Brushes a finger down the seam of my shorts. The shorts are thin, and underneath I'm wearing a pair of equally thin lace panties, so the touch on my swollen, eager body is absolutely electric. My hips lift completely without my permission, seeking more.

"Is that so?" he asks. "You like that? You want me to do it again?"

A very small part of my brain is trying to cling to sanity and...failing.

"Yes" falls from my lips.

He grins, extends his finger, and strokes me again.

My eyes drift closed.

"Like this?" he wants to know, his touch still light. Teasing. Tormenting.

It's not enough.

I shake my head.

"Harder?" he asks, and now it's his palm cupping me,

rubbing perfect friction over every hungry, needy bit of me, and it's good, but—

It's not enough.

And he knows. I don't know how he knows, but he knows, and everything happens fast then. He plants a knee next to me on the couch and his mouth comes down on mine, fierce and hungry and unrelenting. I'm on my back before I can register it; he's on me, a thigh between mine. His hands gather my wrists and press them over my head.

"Yeah," I say. It spills out of my mouth.

It's so good. His lips soft but commanding, his tongue stroking into my mouth like he's telling me what he's going to do to me the second he gets the chance, and I'm all for it. I want it *now now now—do it now*.

"I know you do," he says—because of course I begged him out loud, of course I have no self-control when it comes to Shane Fucking Hott. "But you're going to wait till I say you're ready."

His hands hold my wrists still, his thigh has me pinned, his mouth is plundering mine. He licks and kisses and suckles and teases and works that thigh against the wildly needy swollen curve of my sex, and everything inside me winds itself into a tight, hot knot—*don't stop, please don't stop*—and then I'm coming so hard, my face buried against his neck, the vise of his hand still tight on my wrists, his thigh giving something for the spasms of pleasure to echo off of, so they go on and on—*I've never come this hard in my life*.

"Good to hear it," he says—because of course I've said that out loud, too.

23

SHANE

She's perfect.

Incredible.

The heat of her mouth, the curl and stroke of her tongue, her soft, strong body writhing under mine on the couch.

The fierceness of her response to me, and the way she broke while I held her and kissed her, breathless and moaning, my name and all manner of filthy words on her lips.

It's testament to willpower that I didn't follow her over the edge because I was right there with her, so wrapped up in her pleasure that I couldn't feel where she ended and I began—

And I wasn't even inside her.

We weren't even naked.

She is going to destroy me if we ever do that. I will never be the same again.

Which is why I sit up on the couch and straighten my clothes. I help her sit up, too, and I watch as she fixes her hair and fusses over her clothes and doesn't make eye contact at all.

Finally I say, "Ivy, it's okay. It's not a big deal."

Her eyes flash to mine, and I see relief in them.

"I'm your fake fiancé. Least I can do is help relieve the tension."

She laughs then. "Especially when it was your fault to begin with."

Did I mention how much I liked that? It wasn't like I walked in on her watching some random bit of sexy television. I walked in on her getting herself off to the sight of me fucking on-screen.

I'd pin it at thirty percent ego trip, thirty percent the sheer spank-bank fantasy of watching a woman pleasure herself while she watches me, and—what does that leave?

Forty percent the fact that Ivy apparently has a direct line to my sex drive. She turns me on like no one I've ever met before.

I should have known that when I flew all the way to LA to stop thinking about kissing her.

"Yeah," I agree. "Especially when it was my fault to begin with." I run my eyes over her, taking in all the marvelousness—her pink cheeks, the glow on her skin, her swollen lips, the sparkle in her eyes. And I thought she was hot before. Now she's so tempting I have to fist my hands and pin myself to my spot on the sofa.

"You're..." she says.

She's gesturing and looking at my lap, where, yup—

And she's definitely pleased with herself.

"I can, um, help you with that," she says shyly, and holy

fuck, I want that. I want her help, and I want it right now, and—

And what in the name of hell are we doing?

"Maybe we should…"

I'm not even a hundred percent sure what I was going to say. I think I might have been about to say, *Maybe we should talk about this.* And suddenly I have sympathy for all the women who've ever tried to say that to me, all the women to whom I've said, *I'm sorry, but I just don't do relationships. I thought I made that clear, and I'm really sorry if I didn't.* Or some kinder, gentler version of that.

"It's like you said," she says. "It doesn't have to be a big deal. It's just that, I mean, it does seem like kind of a shame that we're getting married—and *divorced*—and no one even *gets laid* out of that. Right?" She blushes even deeper. "Well. I did just come really hard. God," she says and throws her head back against the pillow.

I groan. "You did."

"I was *not* expecting this," she says. "I thought when you went to LA it meant you regretted kissing me. I thought it meant you weren't into me that way."

"Uh, no, not exactly," I say with a sigh. "It meant I was afraid I was going to do it again, and then"—I gesture at the two of us on the couch—"do this. And a whole lot of other stuff. You have no idea what I want to do to you. With you. In you."

"Shane," she breathes.

"Yeah. Exactly. But." I summon every last ounce of my willpower because Ivy is way too good a person for me to fuck around with her feelings. "I think it's probably a terrible idea."

She scowls. "Are you saying you didn't enjoy yourself?" She gives the tent in my jeans another meaningful glance.

"Hell no! I am most definitely *not* saying that. Christ, woman, if I'd enjoyed myself for another three seconds, we would be cleaning up the mess right now."

She grins at that. I like Ivy like this—playful, sexy, enjoying the back-and-forth between us. I want more of her.

"We *could*," she says.

I raise my eyebrows.

"Make a mess. Both get laid. All the things. It feels like the least we deserve given all the work we're doing."

Oh, fuck me, I want that. I want her, I want what she's offering, I want more dirty words in her mouth. I want to lick them out.

I don't want to hurt her.

"I don't sleep with costars," I say. It's just one of many rules I have for keeping things simple. Clear cut.

"I'm not actually your costar."

"I don't sleep with friends."

"Are we friends?" she asks, delighted, and fuck me again if that doesn't make my chest hurt. Because I guess we are, and that's a thing in short supply for both of us. An even better reason not to do this dumbass thing she's proposing.

"Yeah," I say. "We're friends."

She thinks about that a moment, that smile still on her lips. "Huh," she says finally. "Well—"

I don't get a chance to find out what she's going to say next because my phone rings.

"It's Hanna. She never calls."

"Take it," she says.

"Hey, you okay?" I ask my sister.

"I'm not harmed or dead. But in all other senses, I am *not okay*," she says.

Ivy watches me.

"I don't know if I can convey to you the magnitude of this situation," Hanna says. "Easton and I are out at a restaurant together, and I just got a call from the babysitter that she needs us to come home because—and this is verbatim—something has gone wrong with her TikTok account and she needs a hundred percent of her attention to address it."

"Did you tell her to go to hell?"

"No!" she says. "Because I don't want her to give a hundred percent of her attention to her TikTok account when she is supposed to be watching Eloise! Can you please, please, please, please, pretty please with sugar on top take over for her and let me finish this absolutely fucking delicious dinner and order at least two or three of the desserts on this menu?"

I'm laughing because holy shit, I love my sister. "Yes. I will go take over for your babysitter."

I end the call and look to Ivy, who is watching me, amused.

"Did you hear any of that?"

"I got the gist," she says. "You should go. Take over for her. She was really looking forward to this date. And Shane?"

"Yeah?"

"I'm glad we're friends."

"Me, too," I say, meaning it more than I've meant anything in a long time.

But when I'm back in my car, hands on the wheel, contemplating the starter button, I begin to hate myself just a little.

Because that? What just happened back there with Ivy? That was amazing. And I want more of her. And I'm pretty sure I'm not going to stop wanting her.

So in my efforts to be a better human being, I've basically friend-zoned myself out of what I know would be some of the best sex I've ever had in my life.

"**P**arty favors!"

The exclamation comes from one of Hanna's sisters-in-law—Amanda, I think—as she pulls a lipstick-sized vibrator from a pretty pink bag full of crinkled-paper confetti.

We all dive into our bags and retrieve our own vibes, an array of absurdly bright colors. I push the button on the bottom of mine and touch it to my fingers; the little buzz sets up a quiet answering tingle between my legs. Huh. I've never owned a toy—I've been lucky enough to orgasm easily, so the hassle of tracking down the right toy, procuring it discreetly, and using it without alarming my neighbors never seemed worth it. But now I'm curious.

"Who's gonna go home and try it out?" Amanda calls.

Hanna rolls her eyes. "That mosquito buzz? Most of us need more power to get off, like the Magic Wand..."

She's referring to the forearm-sized vibrator her sister-in-law Rachel demoed to us tonight, along with a slew of other toys.

Best bachelorette party *ever*.

And I *really* needed it as a reward for the epic amounts of self-control I've exerted this week not to go to Shane and beg him to rethink his stance. Not only because I desperately want more kissing and more of his thigh between my legs—because seriously, if that man can get me off that efficiently and that hard without even using his fingers or his tongue, there is much, much more he can do.

But every time I almost go running to him begging for more, I remind myself that I need to be absolutely clear in my head about what I can and can't expect from him.

Can expect: kisses that make me stupid and orgasms that make me boneless.

Can't expect: anything else.

He's just a fake fiancé, and after that, he'll be no one to me.

That's usually enough to sit me back down in my seat, to leave me stuck trying to recreate the feel of his thigh between my legs with every last fluff-stuffed household object from couch cushions to foam rollers (do not recommend).

I've gone around and around this hamster wheel a few thousand times, but in the end self-control has won out.

And luckily, right now, I am smack dab in the middle of the coolest group of women, and I have loads of distractions to keep me from feeling annoyed with myself for letting Shane into—or at least *onto*—my pants.

The party has been a head-clearing breath of fresh air. Literally—since it's on a boat in the middle of a lake. Rachel's husband, Brody, owns a charter fishing business that moonlights doing all kinds of girls' nights, including Rachel's apparently famous sex-toy parties.

Hanna invited all five of her brothers' wives and girlfriends, all the women from Hott Spot, and my sister and Akemi, so the boat is, quite literally, rocking. Brody has warned us that we need to move slowly and not all rush to either side at once. (He also gave us a lecture on boat heads and toilet paper; I got the feeling there was backstory there.)

We're well lubed on red wine and have demolished a serious quantity of food cooked by Hanna's sister-in-law Amanda, who's a caterer. We also all survived the sex-education portion of the program. Rachel demoed an eye-popping (and panty-singeing) collection of items ranging from gels and lubes that make your girl parts warm *and* sparkly to vibrators, dildos, Kegel balls, penis masturbators, and a few things I'd never heard of before, like vibrating nipple clamps. I also didn't realize "clitoral stimulators" were a whole different category from vibrators. I guess one works with vibrations and the other works with a kind of suction? Sign me up.

We placed orders for toys, too, although Rachel was clear that sales weren't her primary goal. She's a sex therapist and sex educator, and she mostly wants women to know and love their bodies and understand how to bring themselves pleasure, solo and with partners. Sex therapist is her second career; she used to be a librarian—"and I still love books more than anything except my husband, our kids, and my current job," she tells me.

"Sooo," Amanda says now, and I sense danger ahead. She's definitely the instigator in Hanna's family, like Nia's the troublemaker in mine. "Can we all agree there are two kinds of lovers in the world? Those who will use these vibes on us and enjoy the shit out of it, and those who will view them as sexual competitors and insist they have to make us come with their own two hands?"

We all crack up.

Reggie shrugs. "Given that Ford and I met when I set my room on fire during a night of 'self-care,' I'm pretty sure he's not threatened by my toys."

"Good man, good man," Serenity, one of Sonya's coworkers and friends, says. "My current boyfriend is in the competitor category, which is why I'm already thinking about giving him the boot. Unless you're seriously gifted in the tongue department, don't tell me toys are off the table." She waggles a finger.

Jessa, another of Hanna's sisters-in-law, says, "I put money on Clark—"

"Shut up!" Amanda cries, scrunching her eyes shut like that's going to help. "You know I don't want to hear *anything* about which category my brothers fall into."

"Cover your ears!" Jessa tells her. "You brought it up!"

Amanda sticks her fingers into her ears.

Jessa rolls her eyes. "I put money on both Clark and Gabe refusing to let those things into the bedroom." She lowers her voice several octaves. "'I got this, baby,'" she growls. "'You don't need any dick but this one.'"

Everyone roars with laughter at the imitation. But Lucy, who's Gabe's wife, shakes her head. "You'd think, right? But Gabe is Rachel's biggest customer. And I bet once Clark saw the power of the toy, he'd be right on board."

Jessa grins. "Worth a try!"

"Sonyaaaaa?" Reggie teases. "What about that big grumpy scientist of yours?"

It's Hanna's turn to cover her ears and sing.

"Quinn would probably just treat it like a scientific experiment," Reggie says.

Sonya blushes fiercely, which makes the rest of us laugh.

There's a moment of silence. I can feel the boatful of women *not* looking my way.

Don't ask me.

Don't ask me.

Don't ask me.

Because I already love these women and I don't want to lie to them, but somehow, *I haven't slept with my superhot movie-star (fake) fiancé yet* feels like a can of worms I'm not ready to open.

"Okay, bachelorette. We hear your silence over there," Reggie says. "You're off the hook this time because you haven't known us very long, because we recognize that you might not have enough data yet to weigh in, and because I'm giving Hanna a break, but just know, all of us are dying over here. Shane Hott. Or should we say *Mavryx*? Does he do it all with his man sausage—"

"Aaaaaugh!" Hanna cries, covering her ears again.

"—and the power of his ridiculously ripped ass? Or will he admit other tools to the toolbox? Don't answer that," she says, holding up a hand. "Unless you want to."

"I mean," I say, "it's a very nice ass."

They all burst out laughing, and I soak up the pleasure of amusing them (and the relief of having dodged the question), while the women get to their feet and start cleaning up the mess we've made of Brody's boat. Brody himself—a ridiculously hot man in torn jeans and just enough leather to look dangerous—has been hiding by the wheel all night, but I've caught him laughing at us a few times.

I notice that Rachel didn't say where Brody came down on the toy question, but I'm also guessing you can't be married to a sex therapist and toss the tool chest out of the garage.

And Shane?

I guess I may never find out, and I'll have to learn to live with that.

I feel like I was in New York City and missed out on half-price *Hamilton* tickets...

When I look up, Sonya is watching me. She's the only one here who might actually be able to read my mind, so I look away quickly, hoping my disappointment doesn't show.

Brody checks in with Rachel then, and we begin the trip back to the dock. When we get there, the women all give me big hugs and tell me how much fun they had and that they're so glad I invited them to celebrate with me.

My sister and Akemi take off along with most of the others, Rachel scoots back onto the boat to help Brody with cleanup, and I'm left standing on the dock with just Sonya and Hanna.

"You okay?" Sonya asks.

Yep, I was right: she sees all. Her expression is warm as she leans over and bumps her shoulder affectionately against mine.

"Yeah—they're just really great," I say.

"They are," she says, smiling. "I knew you'd like them."

And then she puts a hand on my shoulder, and I think maybe she knows what I'm thinking, even if neither of us is going to say it out loud.

It chafes more than I was expecting it to—the thought that when Shane and I part ways, I'm probably going to drift away from these women, too.

It was easier the other way, when I didn't have anything to lose.

25

SHANE

"How are the women of LA holding up with the news that if they haven't yet slept with Shane Hott, they're shit out of luck?"

That's Rhys, heckling me from the back of the car.

"No worries," Pres says. "They interviewed all three of the women for whom that's true, and they said they're okay with it."

"Guys. That's not nice," Quinn says.

I turn to look at him in the driver's seat.

The corner of his mouth turns up. "There were at least six of them," he deadpans.

It's a grim day when even your straight-man brother roasts you.

But still, I'm kinda digging it. It's been years since the five of us hung out like this, and in a lot of ways, nothing has changed since childhood, despite all the time that's passed and the water under the bridge.

We're on our way back from a great night. I begged off

from my brothers' first suggestion, a road trip to Seattle to some world-famous pole-dancing club. My brothers were full of snark about how I should love seeing all those women humping poles because *spire sex*. When I said I'd had enough of naked women and poles to last a lifetime, they started in on me about how my pole *sure had seen a lot of use*.

It felt good—the roasting and the laughter, the jostling and shoving and teasing.

Instead of a Seattle road trip, Quinn took the reins and booked us what he billed as a "Quinn"-tessential Oregon bachelor experience. After an afternoon of axe throwing in Bend—which I sucked at, despite all my stage-weapons training—my brothers took me to the Flat Gorge Rodeo, where we met up with Easton's family—the Wilder brothers—and spent the night drinking, eating, and watching grown men risk their lives, which is a hell of a lot more fun than it sounds. The Wilders are funny and down-to-earth, and they could take me and my brothers to school on the giving-each-other-shit front.

Now we're headed back to Rush Creek—me in the passenger seat, Quinn designated and sober at the wheel, my other three brothers harassing me over my shoulders. Well, maybe not so much Tuck, who's quiet as usual lately. Rhys is definitely the ringleader.

"Seriously, Shane, are you sure about this *sex with only one woman for the rest of your life* thing?"

Rhys is, of course, fucking with me. Having dragged us all into this plausible-deniability situation, he's entertaining himself by trying to trip me up and make me say out loud that the thing with Ivy is just an act. He's been at me all evening in this same vein—niggling, nudging, teasing, trying to open a crack that will lead to me destroying plausible deniability.

"Completely fucking sure," I say.

"Everyone always focuses on that part of it," Quinn grouses. "The *only one woman* part. What no one ever says is that you're going to have the best sex of your life every night of your life for the rest of your life. If they billed it that way, men would be signing up in droves."

"So true." Take that, Rhys. I'm in character, and that's what a guy about to get married would say.

But even as the words leave my mouth, I'm thinking about Ivy's couch. Ivy's mouth. The heat collected at the seam of Ivy's shorts, the softness of her rubbing against me, the whimpers and moans and—

My self-control has waxed and waned like the moon on time lapse camera since last Sunday.

I want her.

Even my best self might not be good enough for Ivy Scofield.

I want her.

She's a small-town girl, and I'm bright lights, big city *all the way.*

I want her.

I suppress a sigh. I don't want my brothers to hear it and demand to know what's on my mind.

"You'll back me up, right, Pres?" Quinn demands. "Married sex—the best sex, right?"

I turn around to look at Pres. I'm expecting the same expression I see on Quinn's face—faintly self-satisfied, the look of a man who's getting some regularly—but instead, he pales.

I remember my impression on the day of Eloise's christening that something was off with him and Kali.

I count back in my head, trying to calculate the last time I saw Preston with his wife. Not when my letter was read. Not when Eloise was born. Not when Quinn's letter was read, not at the funeral, not at the reading of the will.

Huh.

I need to ask Hanna when the last time was that *she* saw Kali.

As if Preston knows I'm circling some truth he doesn't want revealed, he says, "Let's ask Shane! How's it feel to get the best sex of your life, every fucking day?"

Bastard.

I open my mouth to dish it back at him. Shiny and glib, just some more good acting. Something like, *Really fucking good* or *Best sex of my life for sure.*

But then I can't do it.

I can't play the game right now.

Maybe it's that Rhys and Pres flew themselves out here from New York to spend the day with me. Maybe it's that it's been so good to spend this day with all my brothers. Maybe it's the way we've slipped back into old rhythms. Only Tuck, with his dark silences, is not his old self.

I mean, my brothers used to be my whole life. I made a blood oath to them, and even though I broke the oath, I never stopped feeling the connection.

But I think it's something else. It's not just that I can't lie to them—because they deserve the real me.

It's that I don't want to lie about how good it could be between me and Ivy.

Not anymore.

Which means I already know what I'm going to do.

"I don't know," I admit. "But I think I might be about to find out."

26

IVY

I'm jazzed when I get home from the bachelorette party. Riding high. It'll be hours before I fall asleep.

I make myself a cup of chamomile tea, drink it at the kitchen table. Then I go upstairs and change into a tank top and PJ shorts. Brush my teeth. Get into bed.

It's quiet in the house. And it's quiet in my head after spending a whole night with those great women.

Which means I can feel the chatter in my body loud and clear.

I challenge anyone to spend a night talking about sex toys and not come home a little keyed up, especially following a week of thinking virtually nonstop about Shane Hott's thigh muscles and mouth and the way his groans vibrate under my skin.

I reach for the little buzzy vibrator, which I'd set on my nightstand when I went to bed. I press the button on the end and touch my finger to it. The high, tight vibrations race through my nerve endings. Even though I can't feel them anywhere else but my hand, my nipples tighten and my clit throbs an answer.

Oh. Wow.

I touch the vibrator to my nipples through my tank top, and—

Mmm.

That's *really* nice.

I bring it down between my legs, through my PJ shorts and underwear. The fabric picks up and mutes the vibrations, and it's delicious. I hold it there a moment, and I can tell if I keep that up, I'm going to come fast. Too fast. I want to play for a while.

It's a rotten consolation for what I really want, but it's definitely better than nothing.

The tenor of the vibration changes—no, wait, that's my phone.

Shane: You there?

Ivy: Yeah.

Shane: I'm outside.

I click off the vibrator. I don't need to get caught with my hand in the cookie jar (read: my pants) twice in one week.

Can I come in?

Hell yes, he can come in.

I mean, there's only so much self-control a girl can exhibit, and my body is already soft and warm and molten and needy.

And he's *here.*

As I pass my closet, I eye my robe hanging from a hook inside. And leave it there.

I answer the door as I am. Short shorts. Tank top. I know what I look like. Face flushed, nipples hard.

I know how wet I already am.

And I answer the door just like that because this is what I want and I don't want to deny myself anymore.

"Hey," I say.

His gaze combs lazily over me, taking me in. And I know he sees. I watch his pupils flare and his eyes darken. I watch a slight flush rise under his dusky skin. "Hey," he says back. "I—"

"I know," I say, and then he takes a step forward and his arms band around me and we're kissing. His tongue is in my mouth, seeking and giving, and oh God, it feels so familiar and right and good but also so dirty—a slow, teasing stroke, a battle for control. You know sometimes you kiss someone and it's like you were made for each other, that's how well you match?

Yeah. That.

"I fucking love kissing you," he groans out when we pause for air, and then he pulls me inside my house and backs me up against my door and puts both his hands on my face. Just looks at me for a moment. "You're so beautiful, Ivy. I thought you were the most beautiful woman I'd ever seen the first time I saw you. I couldn't look away. You've got this—fuck. This glow."

And then he's kissing me again, like he can't get enough. One hand glides over my throat, finds my breast, his palm passing so lightly over the tight tip, sending that spark of pleasure along the cord drawn taut between my nipple and my clit. I must whimper or groan or move against him because he does it again, just as lightly, and then he pulls up my tank and strokes circles around my breast, teasing but not reaching my nipple while he kisses and kisses me like I'm the best thing he's ever tasted.

The circles never quite arrive at where I want to be touched, and it's making me desperate. I press myself against him, trying to get purchase, trying to get friction. I find his cock with my hip and push, and he pushes back, thrusting, lifting me against the door and fitting himself to the notch between my legs, thrusting again—

"God, *Shane*."

"*Ivy*."

"I—"

"I know," he says, echoing me earlier.

Then he's setting me on my feet and kneeling, pulling my shorts down but leaving my underwear. He bends and kisses me, and my body jerks with pleasure.

"I love how sensitive you are."

"Not for everyone."

"Love that even more," he says.

It's the third time he used that word, and I *will not* read anything into it; this is just sex, just pleasure, just temporary—but I do love that I've made him sloppy with his language.

He bites and licks me through my underwear, and then he tugs them down, spreads me, and puts his mouth over me. And oh my God. The heat, the swirl of his tongue, the occasional purposeful bite of his teeth...

And then his attention is right on my clit, focused, certain, one hand holding me open for his feasting, the other reaching up to play with a nipple, and he pushes me right over the edge into whimpering, weeping, *yelling*, thigh-shaking, core-spasming pleasure.

27

SHANE

She digs her fingers into my scalp and calls my name, clenching around my fingers, and I squeeze my eyes shut and concentrate on not coming all over myself. "It's so, so good," she cries, but she doesn't have to say it because it's so fucking obvious and because it's that good for me, too—just seeing her like this, destroyed by pleasure.

When she starts to come down, I tug her shorts and underwear back up, scoop her up and carry her into the living room and deposit her on the couch, and she leans her head back and lies there, boneless, for a moment. Then she slides off the couch, kneels on the floor, and says, "This time you're letting me touch you."

She's not going to get an argument from me. I'm so hard it hurts, and she's already reaching for my belt buckle. Her fingers look small next to its bulk, and for some reason just that makes me harder. I watch her work it carefully through, and seriously, this woman could do just about anything and it would make me think about sex. She gets the buckle undone, grazing her knuckles over the swell of my cock in my jeans, and it surges under her touch.

A moment later she has me in her hand, and now I've got it, why the small fingers got me going: it's the way they don't quite close all the way around me and the way she looks at me when she realizes it.

"I'll go easy on you."

Her eyelids flutter. "Please don't," she says.

Jesus. "Ivy."

"You know what I like," she says.

"I guess I do."

And I guess I like it, too.

Her hand grips me—tight, a little rough, just the way I want it. When was the last time someone did this? It makes me think about movie theaters and back seats of cars and high school.

"Look at me," I command, and she does. Her lips are puffy and pink from our kissing. Her eyes are dark, pupils blown wide from coming against my tongue. Her hand works over my cock, pausing so she can smooth precum over the head, rubbing the sensitive spot right below. She never takes her eyes off mine, and I get to watch the pink rise in her face, the dark flare in her eyes because she likes it, she likes touching me, she likes watching the reflection in my face of her pleasure. It's like we're climbing together, and just before I blow all over her hand, before I make a mess of both of us, I reach down, slide my hand into her shorts, and take her over the edge with me.

We watch each other's faces all the way through it, and it's the hottest thing I've ever done.

Once we've cleaned ourselves up, she climbs back onto the couch next to me and rests her head in the crook of my shoulder. "Hey," she says, and I'm not too big a man to admit it—I have a moment of ice-cold fear. That she's going to say, *I think you should leave.* Or *That was a mistake.* And maybe it's just sex hormones, but right now, it would feel like a slug to the gut.

But that's not what she says. She says, "I never watched the end of the second *Crown of Spires* movie."

"I distracted you," I say and push her hair out of her eyes. It's a little tangled, and I smooth it again, and then, because I can't help myself, I touch my lips to it. To her forehead and her cheek. She smiles up at me, and—

God, that fucking Ivy smile.

"You want to watch it now?"

I don't care what we watch as long as I get to sit here a little longer with my arm around her. "Yeah," I say. "Yeah."

She puts it on—thankfully starting from the end of the sex scene so I don't have to watch myself having sex—and we watch together. She's warm at my side, sleepy and cuddly. After a while she slides down and rests her head in my lap, and I settle my hand over hers.

It's really fucking nice.

When the movie ends, I look down at her.

She's asleep. Snoring.

Very quietly, more of a deep breath than a snore, but definitely asleep.

Carefully, I extricate myself from under her, replacing my thigh with one of her couch cushions. She stirs and mutters something but doesn't wake. I find a fleece blanket folded over the end of the couch and cover her.

I stand for a moment, watching her. Feeling like there's something else I need to do. Or say. Feeling unfinished.

But in the end, I can't figure out what it is, so I slip quietly out of her house and drive myself back to the hotel.

IVY

"I think I might have done something I'm going to regret," I tell Nia as we sort through the costume closet together.

She stills. "Yeah? What's that?"

"I kissed Shane."

"That's not news, Ive," she says. "There's a viral video of you kissing Shane."

"No, I mean I *really* kissed Shane. And I did a lot more than kissing."

Her eyes get huge. "Did you have sex with him?"

"Um," I say. "How are we defining that these days?"

"Did anyone have an orgasm?"

I wince.

Her eyes get even bigger. "Did *everyone* have an orgasm?"

I press my lips together and nod.

"Oh, *wow*," she says. "I mean, not that orgasms are required, either, but...okay, wow. Was it...?"

"Yes," I say before she can finish the sentence. "Yes, yes,

it was. And that was…without…dick," I finish, blushing fiercely.

She's trying really hard not to grin, but it seems to be taking over her face. "Dick is definitely *not* required," she says, and then, "Ivy! You got up close and personal with Shane Fucking Hott!"

"And he *was*," I say. "Extremely fucking Hott. But."

"There's always a *but*," she says. "And in this case, I'm assuming it's not that oh so fine ass of his."

"No," I say. "It's just—I thought I could do this without hatching feelings, but I don't think I'm that person. You know? The one who can do casual? And I don't know whether he feels the same way, and I don't know what to do. I feel like if I do nothing, we're going to end up—"

"Bringing in the dick," she supplies.

I roll my eyes.

"I mean, just telling it like it is," she says.

"Yes. And if we do that—"

"Then you will be forever changed by your encounter with his magic wand, and you will never, ever be able to have sex with another man without thinking of Mavryx, Lord Extyllior."

"When you put it that way, it sounds kinda dumb, but…"

"Maybe just don't overthink it," she says. "Do you want to stop? Do you want to walk away from the potentially most magical dick in the entire universe?"

"Erm," I say. "No. But I also don't want to be that same deluded woman who spent more than a year of her life falling head over heels for a guy who didn't know how to do anything that didn't serve his own interests. What's that thing people say? When someone shows you who they are, believe them? The world knows Shane Hott is a one-and-done, woman-of-the-month club. He came to me with a proposition; he laid it out completely clearly. We planned our breakup first, and it wasn't even hard to come up with a narrative because both of us could look at the situation and say, *yeah, there's no fucking way this could work.*"

"But you're not expecting it to *work*," she says. "You're just trying to enjoy the magic dick."

"It's probably not technically magic," I say. Then I cover my face with my hands and say, "But his tongue definitely is. Oh, garbage, I am so screwed."

"I mean, if you use the old and busted definition, you're *not* screwed yet, and it sounds like you really *want* to be," she points out. "And you didn't say anything about tongue. Please do elaborate."

"No," I say. "All you need to know is that all the sex toys at my bachelorette party have nothing on this guy."

"And I think," she says, pointing at me, "that that might also be all *you* need to know? Sex that good doesn't come along every day. If I were you? I'd buckle up and take the ride."

I open my mouth. Because I really want to tell her that it might already be too late. I might already be in trouble. When I woke up this morning on the couch, tucked in under a fleece blanket, I lay there for a long time, thinking. Thinking about the way it had been between us, hot and dirty and also so, so intense, like his body was already intimately, completely familiar to me. That eye contact when he'd held my gaze the second time he'd made me come. His fingers had been talented, yeah, but it had been the way it felt like he was all the way inside me, seeing deep down that wrenched the orgasm out of me.

Maybe it was just me, letting myself get carried away, but I didn't think so. And I didn't think so afterward, either, when he held me and cuddled me and wouldn't let me go.

I thought something had happened between us. Something *real*.

And then this morning, when I'd woken up and he was gone?

I'd had to work really hard to pretend it didn't hurt.

"So what happens next?"

"No idea," I say. "We have a cake tasting this afternoon and a cocktail tasting tonight. I guess...I wait and see?"

My phone buzzes in my pocket, and I pull it out.

Shane: *Hey.*

"It's him," I say.

Nia lights up. "Yeah?"

The three dots form, then resolve into, *That was amazing last night. You were amazing last night. I hope it wasn't weird that I left. I thought it might be even weirder for you if I stayed.*

I clutch the phone to my chest, mouth and eyes wide for Nia's benefit.

"Good, huh?" she asks, grinning. Then, eyes still surveying my face, her expression gets serious. "Ivy."

"I know," I say. "I know."

"I just don't want you to get hurt. Because you obviously...*like* this guy. And he's..."

"Shane Fucking Hott," I say.

"Yeah," she says with a big sigh.

I sigh, too. "And he doesn't exactly have a track record of longevity in relationships."

"That's an understatement."

I slowly lower the phone and look at his message again, and I can't help myself—the grin just takes over my face. Hell, it takes over my whole body. And watching me, Nia smiles, too, her eyes fond.

"But," she says.

"But," I repeat.

"You only live once. And if he turns out to be an asshole? At least you can say you had sex with Lord Mavryx Extyllior..."

"Screw Mavryx," I say, grinning. "I can say I had sex with Shane Fucking Hott."

I reach for my phone and text, *What are you doing tonight after cake & cocktails?*

Three dots. A long, long pause. Long enough that I worry I've pushed too hard. And then just one word from Shane.

You.

"I'm not sure about this," I tell Hanna. "I feel like I'm willingly bearding the lion in its den. Seems like a bad choice."

"Nan's not a lion," she says. "She's not going to eat you alive. Or wound you grievously with her claws."

"No," I agree. "But she's going to have capital-*O* opinions, so even though this is supposed to be our cake tasting, it's probably going to end up being Nan's show."

Hanna laughs. "I mean, you're not wrong."

"And she's Nan. She's going to say bawdy things that make Ivy blush."

Which isn't all a bad thing. Making Ivy blush is one of my new favorite activities, especially now that I know she blushes all the way from her forehead down over her breasts right before she comes.

"Can't argue with you on that one," my sister says.

By some magnificent stroke of luck, we snag the last parking space in the tiny lot behind Rush Creek Bakery. As we enter, Nan greets us with a wave and shout from behind the counter, then comes out, dusting her hands on her apron. She's in her seventies, spry and plump with a puff of white hair that's gathered under a hair net at the moment.

"Hi, Hanna! Hi, Shane. Wait!" She reaches into the pocket of her pants and produces a phone. "Selfie with a movie star! Come here!"

I obligingly tuck myself into Nan's arm, tilt my head toward hers, and let her photograph us. I can see that she's cut off half my head, but I don't dare point that out.

"You haven't been in here nearly enough!" she says. "The Wilder boys are in here *all the time*. What's wrong with you and your brothers?"

"Quinn's the only one actually officially living in Rush Creek," I say. "We're not here very often. Only on…business."

She wrinkles her nose. "I know what business you're talking about. That *will* business with that *Weggers*. What is *wrong* with that man?"

I have similar thoughts, but the last thing I want to do is egg Nan on, so I just say, "Yeah, that business."

"Well," she says. "Tell you what. Every time you're in town, come in here, and I'll give you free chocolate chip cookies if you let me take a selfie. I get so many likes when I post famous people! Especially Hott ones. Pun totally intended."

I don't dare roll my eyes.

"You should use your fame for good and make some TikToks about Rush Creek Bakery," she says.

I wince.

"Your assistant could do a few of those, couldn't he?" Hanna asks me.

Traitor!

"Sure, why not?" I say. "Next time he's in town with me, I'll send him by."

"Ah, but they'll only be good if you're in them!" Nan says.

I suppress a groan. "Gotcha. So he and I'll drop by, put something together, and post it on my account."

She rubs her hands together. "Fame and fortune, here I come!"

Given that Nan is notorious in Rush Creek for being stubborn about staffing up for the tourist season, I'm not sure how she'd handle TikTok-level success...but since there's not a huge chance that'll happen, I let it go.

"And in exchange, you can give me a yearlong fifteen percent discount on cakes," Hanna says.

The two of them! They're worse sharks than Preston.

"Ten," Nan says. "And only on orders placed at least six weeks in advance."

"Fifteen," Hanna says, "but only on orders placed at least eight weeks in advance."

I shake my head admiringly as they seal the deal.

Just then, the door jingles and Ivy steps through. And God. It's like she's hotwired to me at some deep level because pretty much every part of me reacts. First off, she looks absolutely gorgeous in an orange dress covered with yellow flowers that hugs her amazing body. My fingers tingle with the need to have my hands on her again, stroking those perfect-handful breasts and the curve that flares from her waist to her hips—and utterly squeezable ass. I want to be back in her house, pushing her up against her front door, burying my face in her pussy.

But it's not just the surge of lust that knocks me backward. It's how simply *glad* I am to see her. Just having her in the room makes me feel lighter and happier.

"Hey!" she says. "Hi, Nan! Hi, Hanna! Hi, Shane."

She looks at me, and the world pauses for a moment because I can tell from her smile and the soft, pleased tone of her voice that she's as happy to see me as I am to see her, and that stops my breath.

"Hey," I say and take a step toward her. Then another. Then I tug her to me and plant a kiss on her forehead, smoothing her hair back, grateful to have her in my arms.

"Aren't they the cutest!" Nan says. "Okay, you two, let's get down to business."

She darts back to the kitchen and comes out with a huge slice of cake—one plate, three forks—and sets it down between us.

"Berry Madness," she says.

Ivy digs a fork into the tender cake. I'm about to take a bite of my own when she slides hers into her mouth. I freeze, transfixed, as her expression softens into bliss. Her eyes drift closed and she hums approval, and my cock gets hard.

I'm not going to be able to taste *any* of this cake.

"Holy *crap*, that's good," Ivy moans.

I already had plans for this woman tonight, but now I *really* have plans.

"Shane?" Nan asks.

I wake from my daze to find both Nan and Hanna watching me watch Ivy, amused expressions on their faces.

I put the bite in my mouth. It tastes like dust. All I can

think about is the taste of Ivy. Her mouth. Her skin. Her pussy.

"Whatever Ivy wants is good with me," I say.

"I want to keep eating cake," Ivy says. It's nearly still a moan. She's got to stop that, or I'm going to clear the cake off the table, instruct my sister and Nan to exit the premises, and—

"I don't recommend berry for weddings," Nan says.

"Why do you give them the berry and then tell them you don't recommend it?" Hanna asks, exasperated.

I half expect Nan to snap back at her, but clearly they've been over this before and Hanna's question is more rhetorical than actual because Nan shrugs and says, "So when they taste the chocolate, they know they have the very best."

Hanna rolls her eyes.

Nan goes back to the kitchen and comes back with another plate. "Carrot cake," she says.

"Which, spoiler alert, she also does not recommend for weddings," Hanna grouses.

Ivy's reaction this time is a little more muted, but I still very much enjoy watching her tongue dart out to catch the last little bits of cream-cheese frosting and the way her eyes close as she chews.

"Wow," she says.

Also tastes like dust. I guess men aren't meant to hunt wildebeest and fuck their cavewives at the same time.

Next up is the yellow-and-chocolate swirl. By that point, some of my sense of taste has come back, and Jesus, that is good cake. Tender, moist, flavorful. Until I look up at Ivy's expression of complete, melting pleasure.

Oh *God.*

Just bring the chocolate already, I mentally plead with Nan.

And to her credit, she does.

"This one is my Better Than Robert Redford cake," she says.

"It's her Better Than Sex cake," Hanna says impatiently. "And it's the cake she was always going to sell you."

"Hush, Hanna Hott," Nan says. "I was baking when you were still in diapers. Let me do this my way."

"Ohhh," Ivy says. "Ohhhh."

My hands are in fists under the table. I have to force myself to grasp the fork and stick a bite into my mouth—

Nope. Might as well be dirt for all the flavor it has right now. I push the plate away just as Ivy says, "You might be right. That might actually be better than—"

"Nope."

They all turn to look at me.

"Give us a second?" I say, shooting a look at Hanna and then Nan, then hustling Ivy out of the bakery and onto the sidewalk, where I back her up against the narrow strip of brick between Rush Creek Bakery and the Smokehouse.

I lower my forehead to hers and murmur, "You've obviously been having sex with all the wrong men. You give me one hour, and I'll prove it to you."

Under mine, Ivy's body is soft and pliable, her chest heaving with her rapid breaths, her eyes startled, her mouth open. I can't help myself—I lower my head and kiss her, hot and urgent, until she's panting.

"Get a room!" someone calls from across the street, but they're laughing.

I pull back, recovering good sense.

Ivy's lips curve up at the corners. "I was going to say the cake might be better than Robert Redford. Why? What did you think I was going to say?" She gives me an unbelievably naughty look and takes a step forward so her hip presses against the bulge in my jeans. My cock surges toward the welcome pressure, and for a second, I have to cling to self-control.

I get myself under wraps.

"You were messing with me on purpose."

"Maybe? A little?"

"God, Ivy," I say. "You—"

I can't finish the sentence. *You're so hot, you're so funny, you're so smart, you're so fun.* "Where are you going after this?" I ask.

She shakes her head. "Rehearsal. But we have cocktails tonight, right? You want to pick me up for that?"

"Yeah," I say. "I do. I really fucking do."

You're everything I didn't know I wanted in my life—

"Just an hour to prove it, huh?" she teases.

"I'll happily take as long as you want," I tell her, stroking my thumb over her puffy lower lip.

She gives me one more sizzling look before she extricates herself and ducks back into the bakery.

I follow her in.

"We'll take that one," I say, pointing at the chocolate cake.

"You can always tell the ones who are goners," Nan says to Hanna. "Can't say no to anything their brides want."

30

SHANE

When I pull up in front of Ivy's house that night, she runs out and climbs into my car. "Hey!" she says, beaming at me.

As she settles herself, she untwines her arms from around the wrap she's wearing, and it falls open to reveal what's underneath.

It's a laced red-and-black corset that pushes her breasts up into gorgeous, heaping curves that I instantly want to lick.

I groan.

"Yeah?" she says.

"Fuck yeah," I say, and that's it. So much for self-control. We're kissing and grappling in the front seat of my car. I duck my head, hell bent on getting my mouth on all that creamy, pale flesh and— "I'm going to leave marks," I say and drag myself upright, stopping myself just before I suck on her skin and leave hickeys or toothmarks or I don't fucking know what.

I sit back up.

"If we're going to make this appointment, we should probably—go."

"I don't want to," she whispers.

"I know," I say, "but if I stand up this bartender when Hanna's trying to get her on board to be a long-term partner? Hanna will kill me, and then everything will go to hell."

"Okay, but will you—will you do whatever you were about to do later?"

"Yes," I say. "I will definitely do that later. That's a hard promise. Emphasis on the *hard*."

She snickers and rests a hand on my thigh, which doesn't help the situation.

I start the car and head into town. Growing up, this town catered to tourists who came to Rush Creek for the rodeo as well as other down-home events like quilt shows and chili competitions. The main street was lined with businesses serving family-owned ranches, circuit cowboys, and outdoorsy types.

Now it boasts stores like Girls' Night Out Gifts and Carol's Cake Shop and Vows Bridal Gowns.

"It's changed a lot since I was a kid," I say. "From cowboys to brides."

I pull into a space in front of Vows and look over to find Ivy smiling at me. That wry, amused smile—the one that makes me want to tug her to me and kiss her until she gives up her secrets.

"What?" I demand.

"Is nostalgia why you dress like a cowboy?" she teases.

"Hey," I say. "It was tough to find these duds! Mack's is

the only place left in town where you can find a pair of cowboy boots."

"And the hat?"

"Stole it off a sleeping cowboy," I drawl.

She laughs, and I feel it all the way down to my toes. I want to reach for her, so I turn away and swing myself down.

Inside, Oscar's is hopping. Nothing about this place has changed, thankfully—not the saloon doors that welcome us in, not the stuffed elk and moose heads over the bar, not the nonsensical music selection, and not the mural of Old Rush Creek in the back: dry-goods store, primitive post office, cowboys, and all.

We find our way to the bar and introduce ourselves to Alana, a young woman in a barely there wrap top and an equally tiny miniskirt.

"I can't believe this! I loved you in the *Crown of Spires* movies. And you're—"

She gives Ivy an appraising look, and we wait for it.

"—the one in the overalls that he proposed to!" she says with delight.

Ivy and I choke back matching laughs. "Yeah," she says. "That's me. Overalls girl."

"Would you sign a coaster for me?" Alana asks, reaching under the bar and dropping one in front of me along with a pen.

"Of course."

I scribble her name and my illegible signature and hand it back to her. She examines it, beaming. "Oh my God. This makes my *day*. I'm bartending Lord Extyllior's wedding! What can I get you guys?"

We both order burgers, and Ivy says, "We should probably have mixed drinks, right? Since that's your specialty? What's your favorite?"

"I call it a Rush Creek Flyer. It's basically an Aviation but with blackberry liqueur."

"Bring it!" Ivy says.

A few moments later, Alana places two distinctly purply drinks in front of us.

"It's so pretty!" Ivy says, cheers-ing me with her glass and tipping it to take a drink. She closes her eyes, savoring the mouthful. I imagine that face in a different context, her eyes closing as I slide down her body...

She opens her eyes to find me staring at her. The corners of her mouth turn up, stoking more warmth in my gut. I can't take my eyes off her. I lean closer to her, not sure what I mean to do, only knowing that the force pulling me toward her is stronger than anything keeping me away.

Alana bumps back up to the bar, and I jerk back reflexively.

"So? What do you think?" she crows.

Ivy beams. "It's really good!"

"Hanna said you wanted a signature cocktail? For the wedding?"

"Yes!"

"What's the wedding's theme?"

Ivy and I look at each other. "It doesn't really have a theme," she tells Alana.

"*Crown of Spires*?" Alana asks.

Ivy snorts. "That's *it*. We need a *Crown of Spires*–themed wedding. And you"—she pokes my chest—"need to dress like Lord Extyllior."

"I'm not dressing like Lord Extyllior at my wedding!" I narrow my eyes at her, then turn to Alana. "Ivy's an actress, too. She was on a sci-fi show. *Bridge*. She's the ship's engineer." I scratch my head. "Maybe the cocktail should be called Start My Engines."

Ivy shoves me so hard I almost fall off my stool.

"What?!" I say, palms up, all innocence.

"Don't listen to him," she tells Alana. "It should definitely be called Sex on a Spire."

The bartender gets a funny distant look on her face. "Give me a few minutes."

"Start My Engines!" I call after her, but I'm pretty sure I've lost.

Ivy rounds on me. "Start My Engines?"

My lips twitch.

She shoves me again. "You're a bad, bad man."

"So I've heard."

The space between us has narrowed again. This time it's not all me. It's both of us, our upper bodies drifting closer together. Ivy's eyes move over my face, her lower lip soft. Her tongue peeks out and wets her lips, and I feel it all the way down to the root of my cock.

I want that mouth on me more than I want my next breath.

"Ivy—"

"Here you are!" Alana announces, setting down our burgers.

We're halfway through our burgers when she returns and sets two identical black drinks down. "Ladies and gentlemen! Sex on a Spire."

Ivy gives me a triumphant look. I sigh.

We take simultaneous sips.

"Whoa," Ivy says.

"That's *good*," I say. "What makes it black like that?"

"Can't reveal my secrets," Alana says, obviously pleased. "Those'll keep you busy for a bit." She points at Ivy. "So if you were on *Bridge*, you must know that guy—the one who just got arrested. Anthony something."

Ivy freezes. "Arrested?"

"Yeah. Public nuisance or something? A band out in front of someone's house?"

Her face goes sheet white. Alana whips her phone out, scrolls for a bit, and holds it up. We watch the reel spin by. Band. "All You Need Is Love." The camera pans...

And Ivy's shoulders soften.

It's not her house.

It's not *her*.

Her face goes from white to rosy. "Thank *God*," she breathes.

In the reel, the cops show up. Anthony, agitated, tries to explain himself, but a cop shakes his head and produces handcuffs, and the reel abruptly stops.

Ivy is laughing. "He tried the same thing on someone else, and she called the cops on him! Oh my God, if that isn't karma."

"In fairness, it'll probably boost his cred," I warn her. "Look at the numbers on that reel! He's going to get what he wants in the end."

"I don't care. It's just—it's perfect." She's laughing again.

When Alana pockets her phone and steps away, Ivy takes a sip of her Sex on a Spire. "Oh God. Anthony in jail for being a public nuisance. That made my day." She looks over at me. Her cheeks are pink, her eyes bright. She's almost too pretty too look at, like gazing straight into the sun. "I guess it might be time for me to tell you my Anthony story," she says.

I smile at her. "Are you drunk enough?"

She considers a moment. "Probably not. But I'll tell you anyway. If you want to know."

"Yeah," I say. Understatement of the year.

I want to know everything about her.

31

IVY

His hand curls around mine, big and strong and reassuring, and I discover that I actively want to tell him.

I want to tell him whatever he wants to know. And I need not to think about that too hard.

"It was my second season on *Bridge*. Anthony came up to me at a party. This hot guy—"

"Not hotter than me, of course."

"Your last name is literally Hott. No one is Hotter than you."

He rolls his eyes.

"Are you actually fishing for a compliment?" I tease him.

"Nah," he says. "I know I'm hot."

I roll my eyes. "Yeah. With two *T*s."

"In all the ways."

"Are you going to let me tell this story?"

But I appreciate that he's teasing me, making me laugh

—because Anthony has occupied such a dark place in my head, and Shane's offering to let in light and air.

I run my fingers through the condensation on my glass, a slow curling script. "It turns out he already knew who I was. He knew I'd be at that party. But at the time it just felt like fate. I was at a party feeling alone, and then there he was, telling me he'd noticed my smile from across the room."

Shane scowls. "It's a beautiful smile," he says. "And I hate that he used it to tell you a lie."

"Thanks," I say. "Me, too."

He's watching me. His eyes are dark brown but with flecks of much lighter brown, almost amber, throughout. They're warm, too. He's absorbing me, and that makes it easier to keep talking.

"We hung out for most of that party, and then he asked me out. We started dating. It got serious fast. He was everything I'd been looking for—almost like he knew exactly what would appeal to me."

"He'd done his research." Shane's voice is tight.

"Yeah."

It feels good to have him on my side. By the time I knew I'd been played, my coworkers were already Anthony's friends. Anthony was one of those guys, the kind who's easy to like. Charming, funny, smart as a whip. I was more reserved. It wasn't that the cast didn't love me. It was just... they loved Anthony more.

"He cooked for me. Cleaned for me. Gave me foot massages, brought me breakfast in bed. Took me out and treated me like a queen."

Shane growls. It makes my skin tighter all over. Makes

my blood feel hot and like it's moving too fast through my veins. "I can see where this is going. He made you feel like a queen because he wanted something from you. Which is bullshit. You know that, right, Ivy? You deserve to be made to feel like a queen all the time. For no reason at all. Because you're you."

His voice is rough. His eyes are fierce, locked on mine.

He's pissed off, arms crossed, fingers drumming on the bar, and I can feel the pleasure of it everywhere in my body. Like a warm shawl, like a big hug, like the stroke of his fingers where I want them most.

It makes me woozy. Or maybe it's the Sex on a Spire—because my drink is just ice at this point. Someone drank it, and I'm pretty sure it was me.

"I...I forget sometimes."

"Well, don't," he says gruffly. "You deserve all the best things."

His eyes are dark on mine, and I can feel that gaze everywhere in me. Curling hot and inviting in my belly and also warm and snug in my chest.

"So what was he in it for? The part he eventually got on *Bridge*?"

I touch my nose. "Yup."

"*Fucker*," he growls.

This Shane. The one who's animal-angry on my behalf. The one who would hurt a guy who hurt me... I want it to mean what I think it means—I want it so much that I'm hungry everywhere.

"So how long did he hang around after he got the part?" he demands.

"Long enough that it would be tough for people to

accuse him of using me to get it. Long enough that I got my hopes up that he was going to propose."

Long enough that I got my heart shattered, that I had trouble getting out of bed, that I stopped wanting much of anything at all for a while.

"And when the producer approached Anthony about whether he could work with me or whether he wanted me written out...?"

"That *fucker*," Shane growls again. "That absolute fucking *fucker*."

It feels good, too good, the growl and the anger at Anthony. I want to bottle it so I can snack on it later. I want to lick the anger out of his mouth and hold it close to my chest, and I want to tell him I want this, him—possessive and *real*.

Real.

I want to tell him I want this, him, to be real.

But I'm saved by my worst impulses by the buzzing of Shane's phone.

32

SHANE

The text is from my dad, and it says, *Talked to Allison today. He wants a decision.*

"Shit."

"Shane? "You okay?"

"It's my dad. I have to make a decision about which project I'm going to work on. He wants me to do the big-money project. I want to do the indie project."

"Won't he understand if you say you want to do the indie project?"

"It's not that. I mean, no, I don't think he understands. But it's more that I feel like if I walk away from this project, I'm walking away from the plan he has in his head for me. And—" I hesitate. But she's been honest with me tonight. I can man up and be real. "Not sure there will be anything left to our father-son relationship if I do that."

Ivy looks steadily at me, like she's reading what I'm not saying in my face.

Then she says, "Tell me about your relationship with your dad."

No one's ever asked me that.

"I don't know where to start."

"At the beginning."

I shrug. "I guess maybe the story starts when my mom met my dad. She'd just landed herself in Hollywood with nothing to her name and no connections, and he was already a star, starting to branch out from acting into directing and producing. He got her jobs and then got her pregnant—three times in total—and then he lost interest. In her, in us."

"Shane..."

I shrug again. "Tale as old as time."

"Yeah, but it still sucks. For her. And for you."

"I was a baby. The part that actually sucked was losing Quinn and Tuck's dad. He died when Quinn was just a baby. I was almost six."

She flinches.

"He was great. I loved the shit out of him. After that we were on our own for a while, and then my mom met Hanna's dad. He was a bronc rider. A total swashbuckler. I was a teenager by then, and I worshipped him. I probably internalized his perspective on manhood a bit too hard." I shake my head ruefully.

"I like your swashbuckling streak," she says, her lips curving in that secret smile that drives me nuts.

"Yeah? Well, I'll let it come out to play more."

Her lashes sweep down, almost demure, and I want to grab her and kiss her, but this story is halfway out and I'm not quitting now.

"My granddad hated him, though. Hated when I spent time with him. When he disappeared—"

"Disappeared?!"

"He left town. He'd sworn he could leave the circuit, but there was no way. He loved it too much. He took off without a note and—broke a bunch of hearts. Hanna's and my mom's mostly."

"And yours," she says. Her eyes are soft, and I have to look away.

"I was okay," I say, shrugging. "The part that sucked is that after he left, my grandfather really doubled down on how all the men in my mom's life were deadbeats. My bio dad first and foremost. And then—then my mom died in a car accident."

I'm staring at my drink, still not looking at her. I can't.

"How old were you?" Her voice is gentle.

"Sixteen. It destroyed my grandfather, and he and I— we went opposite ways. He got quiet and mean, and I threw myself into acting and dating. Or maybe you couldn't call it dating. More like stud farming."

She snorts at that, which is good because the story was getting too dark.

"There was a pregnancy scare—didn't turn out to be anything, but she was really late and she got scared. She came over, crying—my grandfather overheard and blew up. Got up in my face and told me I was just like my dad."

Ivy winces.

"Yeah. I started counting the days till I could get out. I leaned even more into all the ways my granddad thought I was like my dad, and I started planning—often very loudly and publicly—to go live with him in LA. Ninety percent, I wanted that life. Ten percent—okay, twenty if I'm being honest—I loved that it pissed off my grandfather."

"I totally get that," she says. "He hurt you."

"So I went to LA thinking—ah, I don't know what I was thinking. I mean, you can't ask a guy who's never shown any interest in being a dad to be a dad. I showed up on his doorstep with a suitcase. It was a huge fucking mansion of a house. He could have put me up in ten different rooms of that house. Instead, he found me a hotel room that night and a place to live the next day."

"Shane—" She looks like *she's* going to cry.

I wave a hand. "I know. I'm sure I need therapy."

She snorts at that. "I think that's probably an understatement?"

"I'm okay, though."

She gives me an eyebrow-lifted *Seriously?*

For a second, I let myself feel it—the ache, the emptiness, the losses, piled up—and then I push it away because—

Well, because that's what I'm good at. Letting go of things that aren't mine to keep.

"Anyway," I say. "To make a very long story short, my dad took me under his wing, made my career, and—" I stop.

And that's when my inner wall starts to crumble. It starts as a knot in my chest, but it grows teeth and claws and—holy shit. I grit my teeth, but there's no stopping the hurt.

"Shane," she says.

"But that was it," I say quietly. "That was all. We never went to a Dodgers game. We never went to a Lakers game. We never went to fucking lunch unless it was to talk about work. He never asked me if I'd made friends or met anyone

I cared about. Oh—oh," I say with a hard laugh. "Just that time when I tried to make a relationship work with a close friend. April. It didn't, and—well, I was upset because I'd fucked up the friendship and hurt her... My dad wanted to know why I was a sad sack, and when I told him, he said, 'Hadley men don't fall in love.'"

I stop because my throat is tight and dry and I need a drink. I take a swig, and she reaches out and puts a hand on my thigh. And maybe I should just stop because it feels so good, her warmth through my jeans. I want to cover her hand with mine, I want to seal her to me. I thought being wrapped around her last night was intimacy, but no, it's this, it's the way she listens and hears and is still right here.

"The worst part is," I say, "I chose him over my brothers and sister."

"Stop that," she says. "The fact that you wanted to go to LA and be an actor, and the fact that you thought he might actually want to be a dad to you—neither of those things makes you a bad person."

I open my mouth, but nothing comes out. When I finally get words out, it's just a Quinn-gruff "Thanks."

She eyes me. "Just so you know," she says, "I love men who cry." She thinks about that a second. "Men who cry for real and don't just fake it while you're watching a rom-com so you get naked for them."

That wrenches a smile out of me. "Anthony?"

"Yup."

"Bastard." I clear my throat. "I didn't grow up with great role models on the real-men-cry front, so I might need some work on that before you see the day. The ones in my life would have rather cut off their own pinkies. Probably need to move up that *Find a therapist* entry on my to-do list."

She laughs.

I do, too. And for the first time since I went to LA, I let myself be really fucking pissed at my dad for not even trying to be what I needed.

She's quiet for a moment, and I watch her, my heart in my throat. She's beautiful like a stained glass window is beautiful, like a porcelain doll is beautiful, but she's neither fragile nor fake, and right now I just want to be enough for her. I want to be what she deserves.

"Give me a sec," I say and pull out my phone.

I text my agent: *Tell Tim Ernst I'm in.*

I look up to find her watching me, a small smile curving the corner of her soft mouth. "I made it so," I tell her. "I took the job I want."

Her smile gets bigger.

"Thank you," I say.

She frowns. "For what?"

"For...making me feel like I'm worth fighting for, I guess."

Expression softening, she holds up her glass. "You definitely are. You're—" She bites her lip.

My eyes are drawn there, to where her teeth dent the softness of her lip. Lush, a little bruised-looking from the coloring in the drinks, utterly kissable. I reach out a finger. Stroke it over her bottom lip, which softens under my touch.

She releases a small exhale, just shy of a moan.

My whole body wakes up in response, cock stirring and hardening.

Her eyes are hazy, and her lower lip, where I touched it, is still open, soft. I want to lick it. I want to lick her mouth and find her tongue with mine and—

She's been slowly tilting toward me, and now she slides her hand into my hair, tightening it to the point of discomfort, which in turn causes my whole body to knot, my cock so hard it hurts. And then her mouth is on mine.

She's so eager and needy. I answer the kiss instinctively, fitting our mouths together, finding her tongue with mine, devouring her. I cup my hands behind her head so I can get more of her, all of her—because I want every last taste and lick and moan. And she's right there, matching every breath, every stroke, every quiet groan that creaks out of me.

And then she's pulling away.

"What am I doing?" she groans.

And I know what she means. I know *exactly* what she means.

"God, Shane," she says. "I'm being such a fool. I think—I think I should probably just go home—by myself—tonight. So I don't—so I can straighten myself out."

I want to say, *Don't push me away. I'm being a fool, too. I want things I'm not supposed to want. I want things I can't have.*

But none of that comes out of my mouth. Instead I say, "Yeah. Probably a good idea for both of us. Just get a little, you know, head space."

She bites her lip. "Exactly. Head space."

We settle up with Alana and tell her we definitely want her to do the wedding and that she should get in touch with Hanna to pin down the details.

We gather up our stuff—our phones, her wrap—and walk out of the bar with my arm around her shoulders. I walk her out to my car and open the passenger's side door for her. She hesitates a moment before getting in—like there's something she wants to say.

Please say it, whatever it is, I will her, but then she turns away and slides into the car.

We're quiet on the way back to her house, the radio playing country music, giving us the perfect small-talk opportunity.

It feels cold and empty, talking about things that don't matter with someone who does.

33

SHANE

I go back to the hotel, fall backward on the bed, and lie there, staring at the ceiling, thinking, *Shane Hott, you're a bigger idiot than Anthony Fessa because that guy obviously had no idea what a good thing was and you do—and just walked away from it.*

I bang my head a few times against the pillow and then let out a groan of disgust with myself.

Almost against my own will, I reach for the remote, and before I know it, I'm hunting down *Bridge* on one of the hotel's streaming services.

Because watching Ivy on-screen is not as good as kissing her or making her writhe with pleasure, but it's a hell of a lot better than nothing.

Except about twenty minutes in, I realize I'm watching the episode with the engine-room scene in it.

Oriana has confessed to her best friend in the crew that it's been a long time since she got laid. She used to have a lot of casual sex when they made refueling stops or delivered cargo, but it got old. Most of it wasn't very good, which meant that it didn't even always scratch the physical itch. Oriana gets cagey at that point, but we're definitely supposed to think that she's lonely and has a lot of unmet emotional needs, too.

And then they pick up a passenger. A guy they're taking to a planet at the edge of the galaxy, a long trip. One day, he drifts into the engine room and strikes up conversation with Oriana. It turns out they have a ton in common. They talk for hours—montage!—about their shared interests, their similar worldviews. Oriana is falling—you can tell. Their flirting gets more intense, and the eye-fucking?

I've always had a ton of respect for any actor who can convey so much chemistry with just facial expression and small changes in body language. And Ivy *definitely* can.

I can't take my eyes off her face. Off the flush high in her cheeks and the sparkle in her eyes and the hungry softness of her lower lip.

I've seen that face—right before I kissed her. Right before I put my hand where her hand had been moments earlier. Right before I dropped to my knees in front of her.

And I want to tear apart the guy who's on-screen with her.

I don't care that he's fictional, that the actor probably never touched Ivy in any way that wasn't signed off on by two different intimacy consultants. I don't care that none of this happened, that Oriana isn't Ivy—

What I'm feeling right now is so primal that it's right down at the bottom of my brain where you can't drink it into oblivion or sleep it off or carve it out with a fucking scalpel.

But for some reason I keep watching.

I watch while he closes the distance between them.

I watch while he asks her, "This okay?" and she says, "Fuck yes."

Every muscle in my body rebels against the idea of him touching her, but at the same time, I can't stop watching the play of expressions on her face. The way her teeth dig into her lower lip, the way her tongue peeks out to slick her mouth, the shy smile of welcome...and I'm hard.

I watch while he touches her. She's wearing those fucking overalls, and she's all creamy bare shoulders and moonstone curves, and his hands look ugly and rough on her satiny skin, and also, I want them to be my hands.

It's torture, but I can't look away, either. And I can't talk my cock out of being hard enough to hurt.

And I want to punch the guy on-screen with her, who I've never met in my life. I don't even know who he is. Some B-grade actor who didn't even work again after this single-episode cameo.

I watch while he slides down the straps on her overalls. My cock jerks against the constraint of my boxer briefs and jeans, even though the screen is showing me far less of Ivy than I've seen now. I'm as turned on as if she were naked in front of me, offering her tits up to my mouth. And as pissed and wretched as I'd be if she were offering them up to the guy on the screen.

He's lifting her up against the cobbled-together steam-punk engine, and I turn away from the television. Just reflexively.

I can't watch.

I can't see the expression on her face as he fucks her.

And it's right then, as I'm staring at the flicker of light

on the hotel room wall, *not* watching the woman I want to be with, that I realize:

I'm done. I'm done running from what I want, I'm done running from what I need.

I'm done walking away from Ivy. I shut off the TV, I throw the remote back onto the bed, I shove my feet into my shoes. I run down the hall and catch the elevator just as the door is sliding shut. I practically run to the parking lot behind the Depot.

I don't want anyone to be with her but me.

Because I need her to be mine.

34

IVY

I stand in the kitchen, wiping down the counters. Like that will wipe away my frustration with myself.

I panicked.

It was just so...good.

So...much.

So real.

That's the bottom line. It felt real. All afternoon, all evening, I felt like we were two people planning their wedding. Tasting cake. Teasing each other. Flirting. Being gently goaded and poked by the people around us.

Maybe that wouldn't have pushed me over the edge, but then there was the intimacy of sharing secrets. Me telling him about Anthony. Him telling me about his dad.

For a little while, I felt like it was the two of us in this together. Opening up, showing ourselves—on each other's sides, in each other's corners.

Then he kissed me, and I felt it in every speck of myself, like I'd let down my guard and now he was in me for real.

I wanted it so, so much.

And I panicked because—

It can't be mine.

Can it?

I toss the rag I was using onto the counter, lower my head to the cool granite, and—

Someone is pounding on my door.

Hope floods my bloodstream, and my heart drums an answer.

I lift my head, quickly survey myself—still in the clothes I was wearing earlier—corset, skinny jeans, boots. Makeup is probably a hot mess, but—

I don't care.

I go to the door, and one peek through the peephole tells me what I need to know. I wrench the door open, and he's standing there, out of breath. Hair rumpled, like he's been running his hands through it. Eyes a little wild.

"You okay?" I ask.

"No," he says. "I'm not okay."

"What's...?"

"I watched the engine-room episode," he says.

His voice is rough. He rakes his fingers through his hair so it's standing even more on end than before. He looks like he's seen a ghost.

"It's so fucking hot," he says. "You're really good. You know that, right? I can't look away from you when you're on the screen. I *believe* Oriana so hard. She's this lonely, slightly angry person who just wants to feel like she belongs somewhere, and instead she's floating out there at the edge of the universe. And she's horny and scared, and she'll cling to pretty much anyone who'll have her. You made me believe it."

"That's—that's good, right?" My heart's pounding, wild because I'm so filled with hope, but also, what if I'm wrong, what if he's not saying what I think he is?

"It's good, yeah. It's amazing how good you are, but that's not the point. The point is—"

He puts both his hands in his hair.

"What would you say..." he says, very slowly. His eyes never leave mine. "What would you say it meant if I said I couldn't watch it? Like, couldn't make myself? If I said...that I really, really don't want to watch another guy fuck you?"

It's funny how I go hot, all in a flash. Like when the fever chills flash over to roasting you alive in your blankets. I think my body knows what it means even if my mind isn't quite ready to say it out loud—and I can tell maybe his isn't, either.

"I don't get possessive," he says quietly, his gaze fierce on me. Like he's musing on it. Trying to puzzle his way to an answer and the answer is on my face. "I don't get *feelings*. But right now, I could kill that guy with my bare hands, and I might not even break a sweat. Because that's how much I want you for myself."

"Show me," I whisper.

The look on his face. It's like something's snapped inside him and he's reaching for the pieces, trying to put himself back together, and then he just lets himself break. But it's not like I was expecting. It's not my wrists in a vise and his body crushing mine and his mouth devouring me until I can't breathe.

It's sweet. So, so sweet.

He's kissing me and kissing me, but not with hunger. With tenderness. Deep tenderness. And he's brushing his hands through my hair like he's giving himself permission to do something he's wanted to do forever. Saying my name until it loses shape and I don't recognize the sound of it, but I don't want him to stop because the rhythm has implanted itself in my blood. He walks me backward, slamming the door behind me; I steer us toward the stairs and my bedroom without asking if that's where he wants to go because there's no way I'm walking away from this again— not until I've had him inside me.

We sink onto my bed, kissing again, our mouths trying to say what neither of us is brave enough to say any other way. I cling to him, and for the first time, the time we have doesn't feel like enough. It doesn't feel anywhere near enough.

"Shane," I whisper.

He unties the bow at the top of my corset, loosens the laces. Lowering his head, he licks the sensitive skin, pushing the stiff fabric out of the way. My breasts, swollen and eager at the pleasure of being freed, sing at the feeling of his tongue and teeth, my nipples prickling, hard, the sensation rushing between my legs. He flicks his tongue over the tight tip, and I cry out and sag against him.

"There's a condom in the bathroom cabinet."

While he's gone, I free myself from my jeans and bra and underwear. Then he's back again, shucking his clothes, fumbling, hasty, and then he's naked and beautiful, all honeyed male skin over taut muscle, sinking down over me.

"I want to make you feel so good," he says, kissing me. Stroking his fingers over my skin, raising goose bumps and pleasure everywhere. Kissing my lips and my cheeks, my eyebrows and my throat. Circling my nipples with his fingertips, capturing them between his fingers, tugging, then bending his head to lick. I arch off the bed, drowning in pleasure.

"I want to make you scream my name."

His palm over my mound. Fingers teasing my core. Thumb on my clit, light as a feather.

"Shane," I moan.

"Like this?"

"Just like that."

He murmurs against my ear: "I want to make you forget everything except me. I want to be inside your body and your head and your fucking soul, and I want you inside mine."

"I know. I know."

He pulls back for a moment, and then he's there, pressing the thick head of his perfect cock to me. Holding there, his expression wide with wonder, like he's never done this before, and it brings tears to my eyes. He moves just at my entrance, making sure I'm ready for him, making sure I'm wet enough to take him. It's a sweet tease, and it draws so much sensation out of me that I immediately need more, arching to try to take him deeper, grabbing at his back to pull him in.

With a long, thick, sure stroke, he fills me, stretches me, the pressure so good I cry out with it. "Shane!"

Then we're moving together, and it's like the kissing, like we were made for this and for each other. My body is soft and liquid for him, and his eyes hold mine, won't let go. It's so much, so intimate—the thick slide, the deep thrust, his eyes telling me what his mouth was earlier, mine telling him back. He's inside me, we're inside each other, and I can feel each thrust somewhere in my chest, like an ache.

We break eye contact, and for a moment I miss it, but then I don't because he wraps me up so tight, he holds me so close. We're one—the slow, steady rhythm of the two of us seeking together, finding together, tipping over the edge so I can't tell if I made him come or he made me come, but we're both coming, coming, coming, clinging as tight as we can.

35

IVY

He holds me afterward. Ties off and tosses the condom, then comes back to me and wraps me up in his arms, face buried in my cheek and hair. Murmuring my name, tangled up with words of praise and pleasure. *So good. So hot. You're—amazing. God, Ivy, I just want to—*

He doesn't finish all the sentences, so I don't know what it is he wants, but I don't mind because he holds me like he can't imagine ever letting me go, and there's something about this big charming guy clinging to me like he's drowning that just—undoes me the rest of the way.

Shane's so blithe and cheerful, but he's lost so much— that has to have left scars. I'm pretty sure he's terrified to need people. It hasn't worked out well for him in the past. It's easier to tell himself he doesn't care that much, maybe even that he isn't the kind of guy who can.

But tonight he let me in. He told me who he was, and even though it must have scared the shit out of him, he told me what he wanted. Me.

And I know he didn't mean just for sex. The anguished look on his face when he told me he couldn't watch me in that scene with Drake Jennings—

The way he made love to me, like I was something utterly precious, like bringing me pleasure was the only thing that mattered to him.

And: *I want to be inside your body and your head and your fucking soul, and I want you inside mine.*

I hold him a little tighter so he knows that I'm here.

I swallow my fear of what *I* could lose and squeeze him tighter, letting him know that if he wants me, if he wants this—whatever the fuck *this* is—I'm here.

After a while his hands move to my back, stroking, and he murmurs, "Tell me things about you."

So I do. I tell him about growing up in Massachusetts, about playing all kinds of make-believe games with my sister, about how we both got into theater in high school and how that almost broke our relationship because we're only a year apart and sometimes competed for parts. I tell him about my dad's death and how hard it was and how Quinn's ALS drug changed everything for us, even if it only postponed the inevitable. I tell him about being with Anthony and not being with Anthony, about losing my spot on the show and realizing I was okay with that, that there might be something I could love just as much in the world that wouldn't make me feel as lonely and afraid. I tell him about learning to garden and falling in love with it— sketching landscape plans, buying plants, composting, fertilizing, weeding, pruning, splitting, replanting.

We lie face-to-face in bed as we talk, hands clasped. It feels even more intimate than being held.

Then I make him tell me more about him, and he tells me about growing up in Rush Creek with four brothers, about how they played in the woods and made a blood vow to run the ranch together, about how even when he made the cut he knew if he could get away, he would be an actor and how he still feels guilty about that. He tells me about how he and Hanna have gotten close again, how he and Quinn are finding their way back to each other even though they're really different people.

And he tells me about his mom, how much he still misses her, how even tonight he wants to tell her things. He wants to tell her that it wasn't her fault that his dad left, that his dad doesn't know how to love.

"I want to tell her I'm not like him," he says. "I thought I was, but..." He stops.

"You're not," I tell him. "You're nothing like him. Look at what you're doing for Hanna. You've given up months of your life to make things okay for her."

"Yeah," he says.

He hesitates, like he has something else to add, but he doesn't. He just moves closer and settles his mouth, butterfly soft, against my ear, his breath whispering across the sensitive skin. I let out a gust of breath that's almost a moan, and he shifts his body against mine.

"Oh," I say, pressing back.

"Only if you want to," he says, and I can hear the smile through his words, even though I can't see his face.

"Oh, I want to," I say, and then we're kissing again.

36

SHANE

"Morning, sunshine," a voice says, and I smell coffee, and then I'm wide awake because the most beautiful woman in the world is standing next to my bed with two coffees and a bag of something that smells *even better than coffee.*

"What *is* that? It smells like heaven."

"These are all for me," Ivy says, smirking, "because I heard a rumor your personal trainer will have your head if you eat baked goods."

"Give me that."

She does, and I open it to find two chocolate croissants inside. I groan.

"Tim Ernst doesn't care if you're built like an action-movie hero," she points out.

"Mmm," I say. "I seem to remember that you care."

Somewhere during time two last night, or maybe it was time two-point-five—it got a little blurry—when Ivy was slightly out of her head from having just come all over my tongue, she told me that I had the hottest body of any guy she'd ever been with, and would I mind if she licked me all over?

Best. Sex. I make a note: I owe Quinn a *you were right, bro* because if married life is about having sex like that every night of my life, you can sign me the fuck up *right this second*.

Oh, right! I'm already signed up.

For the first time ever, thinking about marriage sends a surge of elation rushing through my body.

Ivy gazes down at me. She seems to have gone out for coffee in my T-shirt and a short, soft skirt. Her makeup is smudged from falling asleep without cleaning her face and then waking up in the middle of the night to have sex for the third time (also wow). There are acres of bare thigh within arm's reach. I am already speculating about whether she's wearing underwear.

There is also a chocolate croissant in my hand.

I could totally get used to this.

She settles onto the bed next to me.

"Are you sure you want to eat croissants in bed?"

She shrugs. "We can wash the sheets. And if the alternative is getting out of bed, this is way better."

"Amen," I say. "Pass the coffee."

The croissants are warm, the coffee scalding, and I'm just about ready to spend the whole day in bed when Ivy gets up and goes into the bathroom.

A moment later, I hear the shower start.

She calls out, "There's plenty of room in here."

I catapult myself into the bathroom.

"That was fast," she says, giggling.

"I wasn't going to wait for you to change your mind!"

"No chance of that," she says.

For all the time we spent pressed up against each other last night, I never got a chance to really enjoy Ivy in her full, naked glory. She's—

Perfect. Gorgeous tits, narrow waist, full hips, an adorable honey-blond tuft of pubic hair.

I step into the shower and crowd her against the wall.

"You're blocking the view," she grouses, giving me a little shove back and ogling me in return.

Then she does something that pretty much kills me. She drops to her knees, the water pouring over her hair, and wraps her hand around my cock. She doesn't put her mouth to it right away, though. She *admires* it.

Which—okay, I'm not one of those guys who needs constant ego stroking, but there's really nothing quite as hot as Ivy looking at my cock like she wants to swallow it whole. I groan my approval and wrap my hand in her hair. "This okay?" I ask her.

She moans her yes.

"Oh, right? How could I forget—you like that. You're so fucking hot, Ivy, and *what the fuck are you doing with that tongue, do that again, please*—"

Pretty sure I say a lot more things, too, my voice getting rougher and lower and tighter, until I pull her to her feet and take her mouth, my fingers slipping between her legs and finding her clit, stroking her until she shatters and sags in my arms, while I rub against her hip and come all over both of us with a harsh, broken groan.

I have to lean against the shower wall for a while to get my bearings. Ivy cheerfully soaps herself and then me.

It's really fucking nice.

I'm still toweling myself off when Ivy calls to me from the bedroom.

"Shane."

I poke my head out of the bathroom. She's toweling off her hair, too, the rest of her naked, and I reach for her, but she resists.

"Your phone's going nuts."

I can hear it now, jittering around on the nightstand.

"Nothing good in the entire world ever started with anyone's phone going nuts," I groan.

"Can't argue with you," she says.

Then my phone buzzes again, and I reach for it. There's a slew of notifications, including one from Tim Ernst. *So effing glad you're on board! Sending over the contracts right now.*

Well, no matter what happens next, at least there's that. And the pleasure of having chosen something for myself.

I brace myself to scroll through the rest of the notifications. I'm ready for the worst: Weggers has declared that our wedding is a fake. The land is being deeded to Blue Iron as we speak. Hanna will have to start from scratch. She never wants to speak to me again.

And then my phone rings. I reach for it. Hanna.

"Hey," I say.

"Did you see my messages?"

"I was just grabbing my phone to look—"

"You're not going to believe this."

37

IVY

"I don't understand," I say. "They want the date *back*?"

We're gathered in Hanna's office. She's sitting behind her desk, I'm sitting in one of the client chairs, and Shane is—well, he started out standing behind me with his hands on my shoulders, a reassuring weight, but as more details have come out, he's started pacing.

It's taken me a while to understand everything that's going on. Apparently before Shane asked me to become his fake fiancée, there was another celebrity wedding, between January Stark and Tobias Bauer, that was supposed to fulfill the terms of the will. Only Tobias got another woman pregnant, there was a big public stink, and—it fell apart.

Enter the fake wedding between me and Shane.

Only it turns out that Tobias didn't get Lilla Thornton pregnant at all. One of her girlfriends came out and admitted that Lilla faked the whole thing for publicity.

"But he still cheated on her...?" I ask.

"No," Hanna says. "He slept with Lilla before he and January got together. He never cheated on January. He was only going to marry Lilla because she was pregnant and he thought it was the right thing to do. But when the truth came out, they canceled the wedding, and ever since then, he's been trying to convince January to give him another chance. Apparently last night she finally said yes to him—"

"And now they want 'their wedding' back," Shane says, air quoting it. "With less than two weeks to go."

I should be relieved at the thought of January and Tobias taking back our wedding. It simplifies my life dramatically. No wedding, no divorce, no muss, no fuss.

But what I mostly feel is...sad.

Sad that I won't get to be Shane's wife—not even his fake wife.

And the sadness tells me everything I didn't want to know.

I'm in love with him.

Somewhere along the way, I let myself fall so hard for this guy that fake marrying him was going to feel like a win —and this, admitting the game is up, feels like a loss.

"Yeah," Hanna says. "They called and asked if the date was still available—"

"And you said?" Shane raises one eyebrow.

"I said I wasn't sure."

He snorts. "They must have loved that."

"I said I had to check on a few things and that I'd get back to them ASAP."

"And we're your few things," Shane says.

"I mean—yeah." She aims a hard look at him. Then at me. "I can tell Tobuary to go fuck themselves. But I need to know you're sure Weggers believes you two are the real thing."

I'm the real thing.

Are you?

Of course that's not what Hanna's asking us. She's asking us what Weggers believes. And Shane says what I'm thinking:

"I think we have to ask Weggers."

"Ask him straight out? Like, do you buy that Shane and Ivy are in love, or would you be more comfortable endorsing January and Tobias?"

"I mean, that's what you want to know, isn't it?"

Hanna sighs. "I guess so."

TWENTY MINUTES LATER, Weggers is in Hanna's office.

"So you're saying you have *two* celebrity weddings?" he says, looking as confused as I felt when Hanna first explained the situation to us.

"Sort of," she says. "They're technically...at the same time. So we can only have one of them. The other would have to be...postponed. Which would put it out of the time frame of the will's requirements. So I guess you could say we're asking you...which wedding would you...er, feel better about?"

Weggers puffs out his chest, and I have to fight to keep from laughing. Only the little bald attorney would take it as a point of pride to be asked his opinion on which of two couples is more in love.

But at the same time, I feel weirdly vulnerable. Once upon a time I was worried that Weggers would see our deception. Now I'm afraid he'll see the truth.

That I'm in love with Shane.

And worse.

That Shane's not in love with me.

Hanna does a recap for Weggers. It reminds me of reality TV.

Couple number one, January and Tobias, met at a party thrown by January's bestie. It was love at first sight, but they'd been tragically broken up by a lie told by Tobias's ex-girlfriend, the It girl of the moment, Lilla Thornton. Still, true love prevailed. Tobias wooed January back, and she realized she couldn't live without him.

Couple number two, Shane and Ivy, also met at a party in LA, but they became friends, not lovers. They were fundamentally incompatible because Shane was a partying playboy who loved his fame and LA lifestyle, and Ivy was looking for love, family, and happily ever after. Ivy was headed out of LA in pursuit of a small-town life, and they both figured that was the end of the story. But then they met up again in Rush Creek, acknowledged the feelings they'd been denying, and found a way to make it work.

Even I have to admit, I find the *happily ever after* part of the story difficult to believe.

If it were me?

I'd buy January and Tobias.

Weggers preens. Paces a bit. Considers his options.

"The real question is," he says finally, "what would your grandfather want? Because ultimately, that's my job. To be his agent on Earth."

I sneak a glance at Shane. He rolls his eyes and grins at me. And I suddenly feel like maybe everything will be okay. What happened last night—that must have meant something to him, too. What he said about not wanting to see me with anyone else. What we did, how it felt.

And it was good this morning, too.

You can fake a lot of things, but not a morning after.

I reach for Shane's hand, but just as my skin touches his, Weggers says, "January and Tobias."

Shane pulls away like he's touched a hot stove.

"It just feels like the safer bet. The two of you—the timing was just too convenient. And I feel like I'd be betraying your grandfather's trust if I let you sacrifice your happiness to fulfill the terms of the will."

Weggers bows his head.

Then he raises it again.

"Of course, if you do get married at another time in the near future, I do hope I'll be invited."

No one in Hanna's office can manage a response to that.

SHANE and I somehow make our way out of the office and into the parking lot. I'm in a bit of a daze. I'm not exactly clear on what just happened or what it means for the future.

"I guess..." I say. "I guess we're *not* getting married? But Hanna's business is okay. The land is saved?"

"Seems like it," Shane says, absently. I think he's just as befuddled as I am.

"And January and Tobias *are* getting married?"

"I guess so," he says. "I mean, it makes sense. They're for real, at least in their own minds."

"Shane," I say.

Because obviously I can't just leave it like that. Not after yesterday evening and last night (all night) and this morning.

Not after days and weeks of getting to know him better and better and liking him more and more with every passing day.

Not with loving him, despite my better judgment and best efforts.

I have to say something.

"It's real in my mind," I say. "I love you, Shane. I didn't mean to let it happen, but it did. And if you love me back, or if you wanted to try—"

His face goes dark. It's just a flash. He seems to get control of it almost right away.

Actors. They have amazing self-restraint. Amazing mastery over their emotions.

If I hadn't gotten to know him so well, I might have missed it completely.

But I didn't.

And I remember what I let myself forget, like a lovesick, dopey teenaged girl: this man told me, from the very beginning, that he doesn't fall in love.

He told me that it hurts him to try and fail.

"Oh God," I say. "Shane. I'm sorry. I shouldn't have—"

"No," he says, shaking his head. Waving a hand. "It's okay. Look. Ivy. If there was ever anyone worth trying for, it would have been you."

We stand there, in the parking lot. A few drops of rain fall and spatter on the gravel, raising the scent of freshly moist earth. A car pulls into the parking lot, and a couple gets out. They clasp hands and swing them, beaming at each other before heading inside. There is moisture on my face; I don't know if it's rain or tears.

"But it isn't," I say. "It isn't me."

He doesn't argue. He just…looks away.

Right.

I twist the flower ring on my left hand until it slides off. I open my hand to him. When he doesn't take it right away, I reach for his hand, spread his fingers open, and drop the ring into his palm.

38

SHANE

Factually, I know LA—or at least the LA I circulate in—has always been like this. Busy, bustling, its freeways a snarl of traffic, its people perpetually concerned with their hair, makeup, clothes, networking, partying—and ultimately, their rise to the top.

But since my wedding got canceled and I came back here from Rush Creek, LA feels oppressively huge. Bogged down in its own machinations. And—so, so fake.

I've caught myself thinking a few times, *I want to go home.*

But this *is* home.

And Rush Creek isn't.

It's been a week since I made love to Ivy in her bed, since I slept next to her. A week since I woke up next to her.

A week since I did what I said I would never do again and hurt someone I care about because I couldn't be what she needed.

Quietly, still in a bit of a daze, not quite looking at each other or talking to each other, Ivy and I agreed that we'd wait to tell anyone besides Hanna that our "engagement" was off. Just...in case. Because January and Tobias had flaked out on us once. But once they were safely married, we'd tell our fans that we'd realized our worlds weren't compatible.

January did an amazing job. Her video announcing the wedding went megaviral. She told the world that we were incredibly gracious and generous and she'd be eternally grateful to us for letting her and Tobias preempt our wedding so they could become husband and wife in the eyes of all their wonderful fans and the whole world. Celebrity influencers picked it up and went nuts over the second-chance romance of Tobuary.

By that point, it was pretty clear Ivy didn't want to see me or talk to me. We'd had a few brief meetings, but the last had ended with her running away, and I'd learned from the disaster with April that I was only hurting her more by forcing it. Tim Ernst reached out to me a few days after our breakup in the Hott Springs Eternal parking lot to ask me to come to LA to read opposite potential co-leads, and I jumped at the opportunity.

I went back to LA and threw myself into Ernst's project. My dad called to tell me how disappointed he was in me. He begged me to change my mind, and then he said that since we clearly didn't see eye to eye on my career, maybe it was time for me to find a different manager.

I said that maybe it was, and we hung up. After that, I didn't hear anything from him.

I also didn't hear anything from Ivy, and I told myself that was okay. Better. A clean break, a chance for her to find someone who can give her what she needs. A chance for me to throw myself back into acting with my full attention.

Except acting doesn't seem to matter much right now.

This is the third beautiful, talented starlet that I've read across from over the past few days, and I can't seem to strike the slightest spark of chemistry with any of them.

It's not them. They're all amazing.

It's me.

A week has passed, and I don't feel any more like myself.

It's like I left the best part of myself in Rush Creek, and the thing that's left here, reading with various potential costars, is just an empty husk.

Maybe that's why all the pairings feel empty, too. I haven't read with anyone I've clicked with yet, and Tim is getting impatient with me and the process.

"Go home," he tells me now. "Go home and do some more character work. I don't feel like you're deep enough with this character."

Ashamed, I nod. I know he's right. I want to make this work. I want to bowl Tim over with what I can do. And instead I'm giving him half a man and half an actor. I need to pull myself together, forget everything that happened in Rush Creek, and get back in the game.

"Joe Abrahms has been fighting this battle by himself for a really long time," Tim says. "You've got to totally get into that mindset. Like you believe you're the only guy on earth who can change this injustice."

I hang my head. I don't want to let Tim down. He's an incredible director, and he's taking a chance on me, because I haven't tried anything with this kind of depth and pathos before. I want to show him I can do this. For him, but mostly for me. "I will," I say.

"Give me a call when you feel like you've got it, okay?" he says. "I can wait. We're not in a huge hurry. Not yet."

"Okay," I say.

I head back to my car. When I get there, I check my phone, which has been on Do Not Disturb, and discover there's a call from Quinn. I panic for a moment because the only other time Quinn has ever called me there was a family emergency threatening to undo all our hard work to save Hanna's business.

This time, however, Quinn sounds cheerful and non-panicked. His voicemail says, *I'm in town. Call me.*

When he picks up, I say, "What the hell are you doing in LA?"

"I was meeting with a potential scientist recruit," he says.

"Since when do you travel to meet them?"

"When they're so brilliant they could work for any lab in the entire country," he says. "But the point is I'm here, I'm done with work for the day, and I have two Dodgers tickets."

It's testament to how bad I'm feeling that I don't cheer up at all when I hear that. I just think about how much traffic we'll have to sit in—not just rush hour, but the stadium and surface-street traffic. Then there will be paparazzi and fans who want autographs and, if I'm especially unlucky, even reporters who'll want a quick interview with me.

"I'm wiped," I say. "I think I'm going to just head home and sack out."

"Shane," Quinn says quietly. "Sonya said you might try that. She said, and I quote, that I need to tell you that I came all the way from Oregon and I'm not going back without seeing my brother."

"You came all the way from Oregon for a business trip," I point out.

"Nah," he says. "I made that up. I came down to see you. And I'm going to fucking see you. So if you don't want to go to the baseball game, we won't go to the baseball game. But tell me where to find you, and I'll be there in fifteen minutes."

"No, you won't," I say. "This is LA. It'll take you forty-five."

"Then stop wasting time and tell me where you are."

39

SHANE

orty-five minutes later, I join Quinn in one of my favorite drinking holes, the kind of dive bar where everyone's too busy drowning their sorrows to give a shit about what celebrity walks through the door.

And sure enough, no one tries to grab a selfie with me or asks me to sign an autograph. It's a minor miracle and one I never thought I'd be so grateful for after spending almost a decade trying to be as famous as humanly possible.

Twenty minutes later, we're tucked into a booth in the back with a pitcher of crappy beer, two mason jars instead of pint glasses, and some truly mediocre burgers. Quinn lays both his hands on the table and says, "Sonya says I'm not allowed to come home unless I get the whole story."

"I don't even know what you're talking about." I'm tired, my chest heavy with the weight of my failure at work. I don't want to rehash a bunch of stuff that isn't fixable.

"The story of what happened between you and Ivy."

"There's no story."

He crosses his arms. "Shane," he says. "That's complete and total bullshit."

Trust Quinn, man of few words, not to beat around the bush. "No, it's really not," I say. I take a generous slug of my beer and eye the bar around us. Tin and neon signs, walls that haven't been washed or repainted since W. was president, a few tired post-work humans slumped over their drinks.

It's the perfect place to tell this story, really.

"The story is in order to meet the terms of Granddad's goddamned will, I needed a celebrity wedding. The one I had on the books fell through, so I created a new, fake one, where Ivy and I were getting married."

"Plausible deniability!" he cries, covering his ears.

"Dude," I say. "We're so far past that. Who would you even need to deny it to?"

"There could always be a reason."

"What, are you the lawyer now?" I demand.

"Spend a day around Rhys, internalize his sick logic."

"I'm too tired to lie."

He exhales. "Fair enough."

"Then Tobuary got back together and Weggers said he bought their story more than our story—"

There was a moment when I thought Weggers was going to look at me and I'd see my grandfather's eyes looking out and there would be some—I don't know, some magic resolution, where he'd say, *You're not your father's son after all. You can, and do, love this woman, and nothing would make me happier than to see the two of you living happily ever after in blissful wedlock.*

But that was *never* going to happen. And pretty much

the exact opposite happened. And Weggers was right—pretending wasn't going to solve anything.

"So the Tobuary wedding was back on, and Ivy and I called off our fake wedding. End of story."

"Right," he says. "That's your story, and you're sticking to it. And my story is in order to meet the terms of Granddad's goddamned will, I needed to work at a reception desk in a spa and salon for sixty days. Which meant I was working for this sun goddess of a woman who got under my grumpy skin like no one ever has before. Plus we were living together. And then the sixty days were up. End of story."

I stare at him.

"Oh," he says with a surprising amount of sarcasm for such a deadpan man, "did I leave something *out*?"

"The part where you and she fell madly in love and lived happily ever after?"

He gives me a hard look. "Do you think you might be leaving something out of your story, too?" he asks, speaking very slowly so there's no chance I'll miss a word.

"Well, I'm clearly not living happily ever after," I say, gesturing to the gloriously grim scene around us.

I don't like the pity that moves across his face like a lightning storm. For a second, I think he's going to leave me alone, but then he leans forward. "No," he agrees. "It doesn't look like it. But *something* happened. The night of the bachelor party, when we asked you how it felt to get the best sex of your life night after night, you said you were about to find out. Sounds like there's a little more to the story than you've told me so far."

"I'm not going to spill my guts on this table so you can

go home, gossip triumphantly to your hot wife, and get laid," I say.

He scowls at me—it's the "hot wife" that did it; he's still a little pissed that I pretended to be into Sonya to goad him. But then he squares his shoulders and says, "You owe me one, though. Not only did I save your life—"

"Not feeding me a known poisonous mushroom is not the same thing as saving my life!"

His mouth quivers, like he's trying not to laugh. "Fair," he concedes. "But I also didn't kill you when you pretended to have the hots for Sonya to get me to finally make a move on her."

"Sounds like you owe *me* a favor," I say, crossing my arms and glaring at my brother.

But trying to win a glaring contest with Quinn Hott is definitely a lost cause. He just glares right back, and his glare is way scarier than mine.

And for some reason known only to the god of brotherly love, I cave.

"Okay. Yeah. Something happened. A lot happened."

"You fucked her."

"I didn't *fuck*—" But I stop, cutting myself off at the *gotcha* expression on his face. "You asshole. Yeah. We—" I throw up my hands. "It was good between us, okay? Best sex of my life. And not just sex. But you knew that, didn't you?"

"I figured," he says, shrugging.

Brothers, man. They suck. And also, they're the best. All my defenses are worn down, and this bad beer tastes really good, and his expression isn't so much pitying as it is sympathetic. And so I tell him the truth.

"She fell in love with me. She told me after Weggers said he backed Tobuary's wedding. And I—" I shake my head. "I can't."

"You...can't."

"I don't. Fall in love. I've tried, Quinn. More times than I really want to think about, and one time that—really fucking sucked."

His gaze skates into a corner before coming back to rest on my face. "Amen. It sucks when two people don't want the same thing."

"And Ivy and I don't. She wants good friends and a small town. Her house and garden and her theater. I want —" I close my eyes, open them again to find Quinn staring at me. "I want her to have that. I want her to have what she deserves. She deserves to be loved. She's beautiful and talented and smart and giving. Fun and funny. Amazingly sexy. I want her to have everything she wants, even if I can't be the guy who gives it to her—"

"Shane," Quinn says. "Has it occurred to you yet that you can't fall in love with her because you're *already* in love with her? Because what you said sounds an awful lot like love to me." He frowns. "Except the part where you want someone else to have her. That's just being a stubborn, self-flagellating dumbass."

I've never actually been clubbed across the sternum by a two-by-four, but I imagine it feels a little bit like this.

I stare at him.

He stares back.

"But," I say, "I'm a professional actor. I'm about to start filming the project of my dreams. She lives in Rush Creek, and she's tied there because she runs this amazing little nonprofit where she helps kids and she can't just walk away from that. I live in LA, and a lot of the time, my time's not my own. I don't control how much I'm in the public eye, and she left life in public behind because she fucking hated it. The last guy she was with treated her like shit and disappointed her—"

"And you're afraid you're going to do the same," Quinn says.

"No—"

I picture Ivy in the parking lot, telling me she loves me, and in that moment I wanted so badly to reach for her, to reach for the gift she was giving me with her big, generous, *willing to try again even if it hurt* heart.

I squeeze my eyes shut tight. "Yeah," I say, before opening them to find Quinn watching me quietly.

He pushes my beer closer to me. "I can't tell you not to be afraid, man. I was fucking terrified. I can just tell you what I figured out, and maybe it won't make sense to you yet, but—" He shrugs. "Don't hate me for saying this, but therapy definitely helps."

"So I've been told," I say with a dark laugh.

"Nothing that happened in our childhood gave us a reason to feel secure. Nothing gave us a reason to think you could hold on to any happiness that came your way. Kids internalize that shit. You internalized that shit. It's hard to undo it." He throws up his hands. "That's it. That's what I've got."

I'm having a lot of trouble breathing right. Because...

What if...

What if I...

What if Ivy and I...

"Hadley men don't fall in love," I say.

"What?" His mouth falls open.

"That's what my dad said after I broke up with April because I couldn't be what she needed."

The expression on Quinn's face. Like someone just told him the earth is flat. Disbelief and scorn and…

It fills me with something like hope.

"Oh," he says. "I mean, he's definitely right."

His words hit me like another blow, but when I lift my head to make eye contact with him, he's looking right back at me, level and a little challenging.

"But you know what? You're not a fucking Hadley."

He points at my chest.

"You're a Hott."

He reaches for my hand, and I flinch but then relax and let him uncurl my fingers and open my palm to reveal the scar at the base of my thumb from our blood vow.

We both look down at my scar, and then he opens his fingers, too, and lays his hand right next to mine. His scar is almost identical.

"We didn't mean to set ourselves up for failure," he says, frowning at the twin white lines crossing our thumbs. "We didn't mean to make this so hard on ourselves. We were just kids. We thought we were making a promise that would be easy to keep. But it wasn't."

I've never really thought about it, all of us agreeing to something that big when we were that young.

"We all got hurt and wounded, and we needed to run from the place where bad shit had happened to us. It was easier than staying and facing it. So we ran, but then we blamed ourselves for running. Maybe we even punished ourselves for running. Maybe you're punishing yourself for running by telling yourself you don't deserve Rush Creek or the Hott name or—" He hesitates, and his eyes flash to mine.

My chest is so full it hurts, and I think of Ivy saying, *Just so you know, I love men who cry.*

Well, that's a good thing.

"Shane?"

"Or Ivy." My voice is rough.

"Or Ivy," he repeats and hands me his napkin without comment so I can swipe my eyes dry.

40

———

IVY

"Earth to Ivy."

My sister has roused me from a sport I've been engaged in all too often: wondering if things could have turned out differently. I've caught myself a hundred times in the last week going over the last few times Shane and I were together, searching for meaning in his words and actions. Wondering if I could have seen sooner that I was hurtling toward disaster. Wondering if I could have said something to talk him into staying. *Trying.*

I saw him only a handful of times more. Later that same day with January to coordinate the announcement that we were generously letting January and Tobias have their wedding spot back, that our wedding was postponed till a not-yet-specified date in the future. Once when I dropped his T-shirt, which I still had, at his hotel. I meant to leave it at the front desk, but I ran into him and—

God, it was painful. He wouldn't look at me. He thanked me for the T-shirt, and then he thanked me for helping out him and his family, and then he pulled my ring out of his pocket and gave it back to me.

"This is yours," he said. "I bought it for you. I want you to have it. If you don't want it, you can sell it and use the money for the theater."

He took my hand and pressed the ring into my palm, a reversal of what I'd done to him. He closed my fingers around it.

The feel of his hand around mine almost broke me. I fled, clutching the ring.

Turned out I still had his T-shirt in my other hand. I cried into it in the car. It still smelled like him, which of course made me cry harder.

Eventually, once it dried out, I folded the T-shirt into the bottom of my shirt drawer, afraid if I put it somewhere easily accessible that I would find myself burying my face in it and bawling my eyes out again.

I slid the ring onto my right hand. Even though it hurts every time I look at it, I don't want to give it up.

I've been dragging myself around ever since, and I think Nia's starting to lose patience with me.

"Ivy!"

"Sorry!"

"Sonya and her crew are taking off."

Sonya, Bella, Reggie, Serenity, and their coworker Mei showed up this morning to give the kids a lesson on hair and makeup. They've also committed themselves to helping at dress rehearsals and performances for the next six months, which is...way above and beyond, especially because they're doing it totally on a volunteer basis, despite all having demanding day jobs. I really love Sonya and her friends, and—

Well, it sucks that we won't get to be related after all. I mean, if there was ever really any chance of that.

That's the thing that's so confusing. It was always fake. But it wasn't. And—I don't know. I just can't wrap my brain around it.

I jog out from our makeshift backstage, where I've been organizing the prop shelves in our new, temporary space in the Hott Springs Eternal small barn. I hug all the women, thanking them profusely, letting them know how much their visit meant to the kids. A few kids are still hanging around, telling our guests in their own words how awesome the workshop was and how they're going to apply it not only to theater but to doing their own hair and makeup at home.

"Just remember that stage makeup is a lot more dramatic than what you want to wear to school," Bella cautions, managing to bite back a smile.

Reggie, Bella, Serenity, and Mei, who came together in one car, head out. Nia has to pick up Akemi somewhere, so after checking in to make sure I'm okay with shutting down, she takes off. Sonya is leaving separately because she has to run some errands. She lingers a bit as the kids grab their stuff and stroll toward the exit.

"You doing okay?" she asks, drifting back to my side.

It's on the tip of my tongue to say *Yeah, totally. Why?* but there's something so gentle and generous in her expression that instead I say, "Ah. You know. Some days better than others."

She touches my arm. "Let me know if I can— I can't say

I've been in your exact shoes, but…let's just say that I know what it's like to love a wounded bear."

She says the *L*-word so casually, like she's known all along, and it's like a friendly shove at the edge of a cliff. I can feel the blank expression I've been wearing for days crack and then splinter.

"Oh, hon," she says. "Hug?" She holds her arms out, and I walk into them. Her hug is perfect, warm and lavender scented and generous, and tears threaten. "Been there. Those Hott men. They're irresistible. And definitely a little more wounded than they want you to know. I *so* hoped things were going to work out for you two."

She draws back to smile at me, and I realize she's telling me she would have been as happy to have me as a sister-in-law as I would have felt to be hers.

"Me, too," I blurt.

Her smile gets bigger, then fades away, becoming wistful. "If you want to talk about it—"

"I wish there was something to talk about," I say. "I mean, I wish there *still* was—but it's definitely over. And maybe it's for the best. I mean, he's in the fast lane and I'm a small-town girl, and I wouldn't fit into the kind of life he has."

"I get that," Sonya says, shaking her head ruefully. "I get it totally. I wouldn't, either. I'm *such* a small-town girl. Fame scares the shit out of me. "

"I tried it once," I admit. "Loving a guy who's career-driven and—"

I'm about to list all the things Anthony is.

Attention-seeking.

Ruthless.

Amoral.

My breath catches in my chest because all those words are perfect for Anthony...but *none* of them apply to the Shane Hott I've met. A guy who will set everything aside for his family. Who'll go out of his way to stage a time-consuming, elaborate proposal to help a woman out. Who's funny and generous (including in bed) and more sensitive than he wants to let on. Who wanted just one man—any man—to stick around in his life, got disappointed over and over again, and still had a soft enough heart to be wounded when the latest one let him down. Who disappointed one woman he cared about—and lost her—and never, ever wants to do it again. Who's afraid he won't be the man who sticks around in someone else's life.

Who's afraid.

Who's afraid.

Like I'm afraid.

"—and I'm scared," I confess, and tears rush to my eyes, pouring down my face, while Sonya wraps her arms around me and hugs me and murmurs, "Hey, girl. We all are."

She holds me for a long time while I cry it out, murmuring more comfort. Eventually I have to pull away or I'll get snot and tears on Sonya's silk blouse. She insists she doesn't care, that it's going to the dry cleaner later today, and she digs in her purse and pulls out one of those small plastic packs of tissues, which she hands me. I get myself under control, and she says, "You know, Quinn and I almost broke up. He almost went back to Boston."

"And then what happened?"

"Well, we realized we wanted to be with each other more than we wanted to hang on to our baggage, I guess?

Oh!" she cries suddenly as her handbag begins to play Meghan Trainor's "Badass Woman." "Hang on—that's Hanna calling from the Bat Phone."

"There's a *Bat Phone*?"

"I mean, not literally—there are no bats or bat-people in this scenario—but yeah, that's Hanna's emergency ringtone. Hey," she says, answering.

Her face goes absolutely white. "No," she says. "Oh, *fuck*." She listens some more. "Yeah, actually, she's...here. And yeah. I can tell her."

She hangs up and looks at me. Her eyes are huge.

"What is it?" I ask, my stomach curdling.

"I don't even know how to tell you this," she says.

"Just tell me," I say. "Rip off the Band-Aid."

Her phone pings, and she looks down at it. Hangs her head.

"Sonya?"

She holds up her phone. It's the front page of a celebrity news site. There's a photo at the top of the page under the headline *A Hot Day for January*. I squint at it. It takes a moment to figure out what I'm seeing. A gorgeous woman in a passionate clinch with a handsome man.

"That's January Stark," I say.

"Yeah," Sonya says bleakly.

"And that's..."

We stare at each other as the full weight of what I'm seeing sinks in.

Sonya finishes the sentence for me. "Definitely not Tobias Bauer."

Hanna has her head down on her desk. I think it's the first time I've ever seen her in what looks like despair.

She lifts her head when Sonya knocks quietly on the door frame.

"Oh," Hanna says. "Hi. I wasn't expecting you…"

She aims that at me.

"I wanted to see if I could do anything to help," I say.

"You don't owe me anything." Her face is bleak, her words taut. "You've done too much already, and—I'm so sorry about the way things turned out with Shane. I thought…"

But she doesn't finish the sentence.

"I'm not very good at knowing what people are feeling," she says instead. "But you don't need to be here. You don't need to help."

"I know." I sit in one of the chairs across from her. "Sonya and I already went over this on the way over. I'm not here because I feel like I owe anyone anything. I'm here because I want to help." I look from Sonya to Hanna and back again. I think of the morning when Sonya and her friends pitched in to make me over for the fake proposal. Of the day Hanna and company spent finding a wedding dress for me. And the bachelorette party no one was obligated to throw me, the one that made me feel for the first time in a long while like I belonged.

I've lost Shane—but I don't have to lose everything.

"I'm here because you're my friend."

Her eyes fill with tears, and I've already known her long enough to know *that* doesn't happen very often.

"Thank you," she says simply.

She sits up straighter. She moves some papers from one side of her desk to the other. "Tobias canceled," she says.

"I figured."

"There are seventy-two hours till the wedding," she says. "Or—until the moment formerly known as a wedding. We probably have less than twenty-four hours before Weggers sees the Tobuary news."

I'd known this was coming, but hearing it laid out that starkly makes my stomach hurt. Because it's pretty obvious what needs to happen. And I need to be the one to say it.

I take a deep breath.

"If you need me to," I tell Hanna, "I'll marry Shane."

Hanna texts Shane, and when he doesn't respond right away, she calls him and leaves a voicemail.

"January cheated," she says bluntly. "Their wedding's off again. I need you to come back here. I need you to marry Ivy."

She looks up at me, then away.

"I'm sorry, Shane. I know this is—complicated. But I need you."

If her tears are rare, I'm guessing a straight-out ask for help is even rarer.

And I'm also guessing there's no way Shane will turn it down, no matter how uncomfortable he is.

Obviously that's what we want, and yet the thought makes my chest so tight I can barely breathe. Less than seventy-two hours from now, I'm going to stand across from the man who broke my heart and say *I do*. It will be the hardest acting job I've ever done—and the most painful by far. And he'll be looking into my eyes the whole time, so even if the rest of the world believes my brave face?

I'm pretty sure he'll know the truth.

Sonya keeps asking me if I'm sure, and I keep saying yes. Because there's too much at stake here to let my hurt feelings rule the day. I knew what I was getting myself into from the very beginning. Shane *never* lied to me about what he was capable of. If I let myself believe otherwise, it's because I failed to learn the lesson Anthony should have taught me once and for all.

"You should go home," Hanna says.

"I want to help. There must be vendor calls to make. We have to reinstitute Plan A. Or Plan B. Whatever the hell I am."

I almost laugh because if you take the broken heart out of the equation, it's pretty funny. But I'm not there.

Honestly, I'm not sure I'll ever be there.

Sonya touches my arm. "We can do all that in the morning. Go home, grab something to eat, get some sleep, and meet us back here tomorrow morning. By then Shane will be here, and we can figure this out."

I know I won't be able to eat, and I'm pretty sure I won't be able to sleep, but I agree to meet them back at Hott Springs tomorrow morning around ten to dive into the thorny details of tweaking a wedding that's only seventy-two hours out.

Then I do as instructed. Or well, mostly. I go home. I take a shower. I stand in front of the refrigerator and stare into it, my stomach clenching.

And then I lie in bed for a long, long time before fitful sleep comes for me.

IN THE MORNING, I get up, shower, and spend way too long contemplating my clothing options.

Do I dress to make him regret all his decisions?

Or do I slog over to Hott Springs headquarters in the clothes that best reflect my state of mind—ten-year-old sweats?

In the end, I split the difference. I throw on a pink T-shirt that says *Inhale tacos, exhale negativity*, my most flattering jeans, and a pair of purple Converse high-tops. My hair's clean and my makeup is the fruit of years of figuring out how to look *just rolled out of bed and I'm always this gorgeous and dewy.*

Let him think a little about what he's missing.

Of course, he's probably not missing it. He's probably back to his old habits.

I haven't let myself search for his name online because seeing him with someone else on his arm would wreck me.

I almost change into the sweats, but I'm running late, so I get into the car.

A few minutes after ten, I pull into the Hott Springs parking lot and head inside.

Since the individual offices are small, we've set up in what Easton tells me used to be the living room of the old ranch house but is now the big reception area of the business. It's a massive great room with high ceilings, thick beams, and a huge stone fireplace. Two of the room's three walls are mostly windows with dramatic views of the Cascades. Despite the rustic architecture, there's a bridal aesthetic to everything—the furniture is white and gold upholstered, a modern take on Victorian styling, the floor-length drapes are the same fabric, and twinkle lights give the whole room a celebratory feeling. There are loads of bridal magazines tossed onto the coffee table.

Our small but mighty crew is spread out around the room with cell phones in hand: Hanna, Sonya, Easton, and me.

Just before lunchtime, Hanna's brother Rhys, the lawyer, walks in. He's clean shaven, neatly groomed, and well dressed in trousers and a dress shirt. You can't miss the Hott family resemblance, and my stomach pitches.

Shane's still not here.

Everyone seems to assume he's coming—but he hasn't replied to my terse text telling him that I'll do whatever needs to be done to help Hanna.

I don't say, *including marrying you*. I think it's obvious.

Hanna is tied up talking on the phone to January, who has been calling her in tears since the news broke yesterday. As Rhys approaches her, Hanna wraps an arm around his midsection and gives him a sideways hug without ending the call. A few minutes later, though, she hangs up and hugs him in earnest.

"What are you doing here!?"

"Flew in to help," he says.

She lets him go and turns to me. "This is my brother Rhys," she tells us proudly.

"It's a fake," he says bluntly.

"*What?*"

"The photo. It's a fake. A really good deepfake. I've got several contacts who are experts in deepfakes, so I ran it by them. With AI, this is coming up more and more in family law cases, so I've been collecting experts. I got their responses when I was in the car on the way from the airport. All three of them said basically the same thing. Real January doesn't have a tattoo on her wrist—her character in *Salient* did, but it was a temporary. And if you look at how they're posed, she's in the same position, more or less, as one of the steamy scenes in *Salient*." He holds up his phone to show us a video still and the photo of January.

"Holy *shit*," Hanna breathes, color coming back into her face for the first time since the apparently fake January news broke.

"God," I say. "That's—really disturbing. I mean, speaking as the resident actress. This is my worst nightmare come true—that someone mashes up reality and fiction and smears me."

"And it's not that hard to do," Rhys says. "The technology is basically everywhere now."

Frowning, Hanna says, "Who would bother to fake a photo like that?"

Easton sighs. "A lot of people," he says. "Hollywood enemies. Press looking to capitalize on a good story." He ponders for a moment. "Someone who had something to gain by keeping the wedding from happening."

"Weggers," Hanna growls.

Sonya looks at Rhys, a question in her eyes. "Does he? I know he's a pain in the ass, but sabotage?"

"Seems unlikely," he admits. "He's a pain in the ass, not an evil genius. And can you see him deepfaking a photo?"

"God, Rhys," Hanna says, handing the phone back to him. "I don't know whether to thank you or hate you right now. But I know January is going to be extremely grateful."

That's when her gaze snaps to my face. Along with pretty much everyone else's in the room.

That's when it hits me: it's really, truly all over.

Wedding saved. Crisis averted.

I'm not needed.

"I guess I'll just…" I edge a thumb in the direction of the doorway.

Sonya takes a step toward me. Hanna, too.

"It's okay," I say. "I'm *fine*. It's better this way."

The looks on their faces say they don't believe me. But it's true. The only thing that could make me feel worse than I feel right now is to have to stand face-to-face with Shane while we lie to the world.

"Ivy," Sonya says.

"It's okay," I say. "I just need to—go."

Sonya gives me a swift, hard hug. Hanna, too.

And then I go. I walk out the front door of Hott Springs, down the front steps, and into the parking lot.

Just as a BMW convertible pulls in.

My stomach turns over, and that tightness in my chest —which never really left—comes back with a vengeance.

Shane is behind the wheel.

He emerges from the car—tall, golden, and so painfully familiar.

God, he looks good. It hurts to look at him, at the tousled hair and the strong jaw, the full lips, the broad shoulders. The way his sage-green T-shirt clings to the thick muscles of his upper arms, leaving his tapered forearms bare.

But whatever. I've seen so many good-looking men who weren't worth the paper they were printed on. I can steel myself against this one, too.

I'm an actress, after all.

"Ivy," he says, striding toward me, "we need to talk."

I shake my head. "No. We don't. There's nothing to talk about. It was a fake—the January photo was a fake. The Tobuary wedding's back on. So we're off the hook."

He opens his mouth, but I cut him off. "Look. Let's not make this any harder than it has to be. You don't have to say anything. I'm a big girl. I know you're here to help Hanna. Me, too. And we got lucky. We don't have to fake it anymore. We're done."

He shakes his head, his face clouded with confusion. "Ivy, what are you *talking* about?"

"The wedding," I say. "Tobias and January are back on. We're off. And that's a good thing. Because I don't think I could do that again. Go through that again. Let you wreck me again—"

I have to stop because I'm breathing hard, tears surging to the surface, and the last thing, the very last thing I want is for him to see how very, very much he hurt me—

But the way he's looking at me, so tenderly, like he *cares…*

I turn away, and I'm about to flee to the safety of my car when he grabs my arm and spins me back toward him.

"Ivy," he says. "You said 'back on.' Did something happen to Tobuary's wedding again?"

I stare at him. "That's why you're here, isn't it? Because Tobias caught January cheating and canceled the wedding. And Hanna called you to fly up and step back in—"

He's shaking his head. "No," he says. "I don't know what you're talking about. I didn't fly up here because of Tobias and January."

"But Hanna. She texted and called last night. About the wedding."

"I was out with Quinn last night in LA. He came to see me. I put my phone on Do Not Disturb because...well, because I was a head case and I needed to do some serious thinking," he says. "And then my thinking took me to the airport at the crack of dawn, and I accidentally stowed my phone in my checked luggage...and I don't know, next thing I knew, I was here. So whatever you're talking about, I don't know anything about it." He shakes his head again, takes a step toward me. He still has that same tender expression on his face, like he can see into me. Like he can see through me to the part of him that's missed him so much.

I let myself grab onto a tiny, slender thread of hope.

He didn't come for the wedding. He...

"I came for you," he says. "I'm here *for you*. I stopped at your house, then the theater, and Nia said you were here, so... *I'm* here because—I don't want to lose you. I want what we have together...to be real."

The vise around my chest, for the first time in a couple of days, loosens. I draw what feels like the first full breath in forever. And that, unfortunately, is it for me.

"You hurt me so much," I say and burst into tears.

42

SHANE

er tears hit me full in the chest.

"Oh God, Ivy, I'm so sorry," I say and reach for her. I don't know if she'll come. I don't know if she'll be able to forgive me for being so slow to understand what she means to me. But holy shit, I hope so. I've never wanted anything as much as I want this. "I've been so stubborn and ridiculous and—wrong. What I said...about how I can't try. I— The thing is I don't have to try. I don't have to try to love you. I'm already there." I take a breath. "I love you."

And it's not hard at all. I thought saying those words would be a challenge, but it turns out to be the easiest thing I've ever done.

Except she doesn't step into my arms. She just...looks up at me through her tears, and my chest splits open.

I'm too late. I can't fix this. It's all over.

I've hurt her, and I hate that. I hate it so much. And I deserve for her to walk away now and not look back.

"You don't believe me," I say. "I don't blame you. But it's true. I don't know exactly when it happened. I wish I did, so I could look back at that moment and say, *That was when I knew I loved Ivy.* But I think I've loved you since I met you. I remember running into you at the spa, and it was like walking into a wall, Ivy. You were beautiful, but it was the smile that fucking killed me. I wanted to know your secrets. I wanted you to smile at me. I'm the luckiest man in the world because you smiled at me—even once. I hope I can convince you to smile at me again, but if I can't...well, I'm still the luckiest man."

"Shane."

I'm so sure she's going to say it's too late, it's not enough, and I can't hear that, so I keep going.

"Then I saw you the day of the Hott Spot grand opening with Quinn, hugging him and smiling at him—and... remember I told you I wasn't possessive?"

"I remember," she says.

"I'm possessive *of you*," I say. "I wanted to dismember him."

"That would have been excessive," she says dryly. And for the first time, I hear a smile in her voice.

"Part of me wishes I'd never asked you to fake marry me because maybe then I would have done this right the first time. Made it real the first time. So when we flirted in the Depot bar, you would have known I could barely keep it in my pants. And when you walked into the room as Oriana, you would have known it was really me, Shane, losing my fucking head over you. When I kissed you, you would have known I couldn't help myself, and when I kissed you again you would have known I wanted to do it for hours while I buried myself in you—" My voice breaks. "Oh God, Ivy, I—"

I realize what the hard thing to say really is.

"I was scared I'd screw it up," I say, and then—

Well, fuck.

"I hope you meant it when you said you love men who cry."

Now she smiles. Really smiles.

"Come here," I say helplessly, my voice wrecked, and this time she does. I wrap my arms around her and hold on as tight as I can. She feels so good in my arms. So right, so familiar. So perfect.

"Shane," she says, and then she's tilting her face up, drawing mine down, kissing me all over until she finds my mouth. Hers is soft and open, forgiving and eager, and I kiss her like I can't get enough. I can't get enough. I'm starving for her, my arms wrapping her tight, my mouth tilting for the perfect angle so I can have more of her. All of her.

Before I've had enough, though, she draws back.

"Shane," she says again. "I love you, too. And I was scared, too. If I hadn't been so scared, I maybe would have guessed in the parking lot that you were scared, and maybe I would have fought harder for us. But I just thought I'd been a fool, like I'd been with Anthony. It didn't occur to me—" She stops.

"That I was the fool?"

She grins at me. "Well, yeah, kind of." She touches my hair, my cheek, my shoulder. Then she's running her hands over my arms like she's trying to prove to herself that I'm real, like she can't get enough. "I don't know when I started loving you, either."

I shrug. "It doesn't matter that much. But you should know that I don't plan to stop."

"Me neither," she says.

My eyes go to her mouth, which I've missed so much, and I lower mine to hers, and then we're both so fucking gone, devouring each other. She's whimpering and moaning and murmuring, "You know what the best way is if you want me to really believe you love me."

"What?" I ask.

"You're going to have to show me."

"Huh," says a voice behind us. "Okay. So. Misjudged *that* one."

We turn to find Weggers standing behind us.

"How long have *you* been there?" I groan.

He tilts his bald head. "Just since Ivy said she loved you. Parked over by the lodge and walked over here. You two didn't even hear me, you were so..." He waves a hand at the two of us. "Huh," he says again. "Well." He seems genuinely surprised but not, I note, displeased. "I think your grandfather would approve."

"You know I don't give a shit, right?" I say.

He stares at us a moment longer. "Tell me one thing," he says. "Were you faking? In the beginning?"

We look at each other.

"No," we say at the same time.

Weggers tilts his head and gives us one last hard look. Then he swivels on a heel and heads up to the main Hott Spring office building, aka the ranch house.

A moment later Hanna pokes her head out the front door.

"You guys!" she calls. "Quit making up and making out in my parking lot. Get the hell out of here!"

I grin at Ivy. "I guess the showing you starts right now."

I scoop her up in my arms and carry her to my car.

43

IVY

"I never stopped thinking about you," Shane says. "I never stopped wanting you. I never stopped imagining this."

We're kissing just inside my front door, which is as far as we made it before Shane's lips found mine. Before his tongue begged me for entrance and I let him in, the two of us groaning into each other's mouths, our bodies fusing from chest to thigh. I staggered back against the door, and he pinned me there, lifting me so I could feel his hard heat against the neediest part of me, so I could rub myself against him, whimpering, until he cursed and blurted out those words.

"Me neither," I tell him.

We kiss like we can't get enough of each other, hands groping and grasping like we're worried the other's going to get away, but the thing is, it's almost the opposite. It's this deep relief. This is the first time I'm not afraid.

And it feels so good that I want to tell him. I want him to know.

I break the kiss and say, "You know what's so good about this?"

"What?" he asks, smiling at me. Grinning at me. I've seen all kinds of Shane smiles, but this is something else entirely, this grin that's like mine when I discover a new peony variety. And I know I'm doing it, too, my grin echoing right back at him.

"This is the first time we both know for sure it's real."

He freezes, and his smile melts away. But it's not gone—it's just changed into something else. A look of wonder. Of—awe. Like it hadn't occurred to him, not yet, what this would mean.

But then he says, "I knew what I felt was real. I just didn't—"

He stops. Cups my chin in his hand. Looks into my eyes, his dark and wild with something I haven't seen there before. "I just didn't believe you were mine to have."

"I am."

The next kiss is different. Desperate, yes, but careful, too. Like he's sampling what *real* tastes like in my mouth. And I'm doing the same thing. It's good, so good. Everything's the same—the heat of his mouth, the eager, needy slide of our tongues, his broken, hungry breaths and near grunts, my whimpers and moans. The way our hands grasp and tug at each other's clothing like we can't get enough. But everything's different, too. How *real* feels. How *we* feel when we're real.

How it feels to believe *he's* mine to have.

The kiss gentles and slows and becomes an ebb and flow, and my whole body feels like it's melting. I'm losing definition and giving myself over to him and *this* and *us*.

He carries me up the stairs like I weigh nothing, then stands me up next to the bed and peels my clothes off with the care and attention you'd give a work of art. Like he's sculpting me. He takes his own clothes off, too, and then he *is* sculpting me, touching me with so much intensity—running a finger along the line of my cheekbone, down my throat, between my breasts, trailing it back up to spiral in toward one nipple and then the other. When my knees buckle he catches me and holds me against him, and he uses those sculptor hands to cup and lift my breasts, ducking his head to kiss and lick, slow at first but then fierce, hot mouth suckling as he keeps one hand behind me so I don't melt into a pool at his feet.

I can feel the strong, deep tug all the way down into my core, and it's tightening me, winding me up, getting me ready for what comes next, which feels like it will be too much and not enough all at once. "Shane," I beg. "I need you."

"Lie down," he instructs. "Condoms still in the bathroom cabinet?"

All I can do is nod.

He's gone and back before I can mourn the loss of his heat, tearing the packet and slipping it on.

"Sword, meet sheath," I tease. "I think you once told me there was no such thing as a sword that's too big—just a guy who hasn't taken his time the way he should?"

His eyes on me are dark and deliberate.

"You need more time?" he rumbles—his turn to tease. "Because I can touch you like this for *hours*."

"Hell no," I say. "Get over here right now."

He does, covering my body with his. He's warm, and I

love the contrast between the parts of him that are smooth and the parts that are covered with just the right amount of hair—like his thighs, now between mine as he nudges my entrance. He drops his head and begins kissing me again, and this is how it is with us: serious and funny and trivial and profound, laughing and kissing, and we get to keep doing it. No expiration date, no rules, no pretending.

An ache blooms in my chest, and somehow it gets tied into all the other things. The way my mouth hungers for his and the hollow sensation in my low belly and the emptiness in my core that needs him and I say, "Please, Shane. Please."

We're kissing and kissing as he slowly thrusts into me. Filling me, stretching me. He moves slowly, almost languidly, and it's too much and not enough. "Shane," I moan, and he drops his head to my shoulder and buries his face in my neck. We find a shared rhythm, the hitch and drag of his hips over mine sending friction to my clit, his cock touching that deep, needy spot inside, and I'm winding up to an orgasm that feels like it might destroy me. I know he's close, too, because when I squeeze my muscles, he pulses in my grip. Neither of us is going to last long, but that's okay because we can do it again and again and again.

"God," he says, breaking away. "Ivy."

"I know," I whisper.

"It's so good."

"I know."

"I want to do it all night, but—"

"I *know*," I groan as his hips grind up over *that* spot again and then again, and—

I'm coming, crying out, pulling him into me, holding on

to him with my arms wrapped tight, whimpering his name and clutching him, and then he is too, deep and still and groaning my name.

And when we're both quiet, he says, with a kind of awe, "And I thought it couldn't get any better."

44

SHANE

We lie together on Ivy's bed, boneless, legs intertwined. Ivy's head is on my shoulder, her arm thrown across my chest, her hair, well, everywhere.

"That was the best sex I've ever had," I say. "But you know what? It gets better every time. Every time with you is the best sex I've ever had."

"Me, too," she whispers.

I'm looking forward to later—and tomorrow morning and the day after and the day after that and...

Well, all the days after that.

Which brings me to some important points.

"In the *fake* story," I remind her, "we said that we couldn't make this work because you were committed to being here in Rush Creek and I was committed to being in Hollywood. And there will be times when I can't be here because I have to be on location or in LA. But there will be lots of times when I can be here. If..." I hesitate. "If you want me to be."

She props herself up on an elbow. "Like—your home would be Rush Creek?"

"Like my home would be Rush Creek," I affirm. "I'd be gone sometimes…but from now on, I only want to take parts I'm really excited about, so it wouldn't be all the time or even most of the time."

"I can travel, you know," she says. "Nia and I run the theater together, and she and Akemi travel. I could take my turn."

I smile at that. "You could."

"I could visit you on location. Stay with you sometimes."

"You definitely could. And I could volunteer with the theater when we're here. I'd like to work with high schoolers. I could teach them acting skills and talk about how stage is different from screen and get them pointed in the right direction if they're serious about acting long term."

"That would be amazing."

"And if you *wanted* to look at TV again—"

She stiffens a bit, then sighs heavily. And she says something I wasn't expecting at all. "I might," she admits. "I might." The corners of her mouth turn up. "But no matter how good the opportunity is it wouldn't be half as fun as playing opposite you."

We smile at each other. No, we *grin* at each other, batshit, stupid, in-love grins.

Which is when my phone jumps and jangles on the night table.

I groan.

"You'd better get it," she says. "For all you know, Tobuary's wedding just broke up again."

I wish that didn't sound like a plausible notion. I reach for the phone. It *is* Hanna—but it's not about Tobuary.

"My sister and Easton are making dinner for everyone. She wants me there in twenty minutes and says I need to bring you. It doesn't sound like it's negotiable?"

Ivy snickers.

"She says, *For fuck's sake don't change your clothes.*"

Ivy glances down at our naked bodies. "Pretty sure she doesn't mean that," she says, giggling.

"Pretty sure she doesn't," I agree.

"Twenty minutes," she says, her hand sliding down from its spot on my chest to a position about a foot lower. "That gives us just enough time to…"

THE ONLY REALLY BAD thing about showing up at Hanna and Easton's cute little cottage fresh out of bed is the knowing glances everyone gives us. But I'm pretty sure neither of us minds because we just had the best sex ever.

Again.

Easton's made a ginormous batch of really incredible meat sauce and several pots of spaghetti and a garden salad with loads of veggies. We heap our plates high and plop down in their living room. There aren't enough chairs for everyone, so Ivy and I take one for the team and cram ourselves into a big armchair together. Other people sit on the floor and lean against the couch or drag dining room chairs in and circle them up. Sonya's dog, Gus, and Reggie's dog, Wags, circle the room, competing for goofiest canine status, nudging their heads against our legs and shoulders, begging for scraps, until Gus settles down and curls himself around Eloise's bouncy chair, his head tuft bobbing like the feathered cap on a Buckingham Palace guard.

Hanna stands up, dings a fork against a glass, and says, "Hey, everyone. I think you all know pretty words aren't my strong suit, but I wanted to say thank you for—well, for everything. For being my family and friends, for showing up, for being ready to do anything to save this wedding if necessary—which also means saving our family's land and my business. Maybe I could have pulled this off without all this help, but it would have been a lot harder and a lot scarier, and I'm so glad I didn't have to. I—I love you guys."

"We love you, too!" Sonya calls out, and there are echoes from around the room.

Shane leans over and whispers into my ear: "I've seen my siblings all in one room more times this last year than any other time since my mom's funeral. My grandfather was a hard man. He never made any of our lives any easier. I don't approve of his tactics, but he gave me my family back, and he gave me you. I can't hate him."

"Shane," Rhys singsongs.

"Shit," he says. "Did I say having all my brothers in one room was a *good* thing?"

"I think I speak for all the Hott brothers when we say we're so glad to finally meet your fiancée."

Beside me, Ivy flinches, and I realize:

In all of this?

We've never discussed the status of our engagement.

I flick my glance at her hand. Yup. Ring's there, on the ring finger of her right hand. Sparkling in the low light of Hanna's living room.

"Rhys," Hanna chides. "Cut them some slack. It was a *fake* engagement. They're not actually engaged." Then her eyes get really big. "Are you?"

Trust Hanna to make things slightly worse while trying to make them better.

Before I can say anything, Ivy says, "Uh, we haven't actually talked yet about whether— We've really only just—"

I don't think. I just...act. Not the fake kind. The real kind, where your heart knows exactly what it wants, where the decision is made before your brain can step through all the pros and cons and whys and wherefores.

"Yes," I blurt. "That's my ring on her finger, and I intend to keep it there."

Ivy's eyes meet mine, huge and surprised. And even in the face of her shock, my heart is steadfast. I stare back, level and sure, holding her gaze.

"Can you all excuse us for a second?" she asks.

Oh, *shit.*

I hear some *oh, shit* echoes rumble around the room as she drags me out of the living room, up the stairs, and into the nearest empty room—which I recognize as Hanna and Easton's bedroom, from the time Hanna spent on bed rest lying in this bed. She pushes the door shut behind us and turns on me.

I expect anger.

I expect a lecture.

I get ready to apologize for being an alphahole. To walk it back and tell her that of course this can wait till she's ready.

I open my mouth to do all of the above, but before I can

get a single word out, she says, "Wrap your hands around my wrists, put my hands over my head, and say it again."

Relief sweeps me, followed by a wave of raging lust because holy *shit*, that's hot. A moment later, my hands are around her wrists, her hands are over her head, and I'm growling into her ear, "That's my ring on your finger, and I intend to keep it there."

She whimpers.

I crowd my body against hers. She's wearing a small, flippy skirt (she did not obey Hanna's instructions about not changing her clothes), and I reach under and tug her panties to the side. Her hands are on my belt buckle, then my zipper, then reaching cool and sure into my boxer briefs, finding me rock hard.

There's a pounding on the door outside.

"No sex in my bedroom!" Hanna says.

There's a chorus of laughter from my brothers, hoots and hollers and more pounding.

"Go Shane! Go Shane!"

"I hate you all!" I groan.

But I don't. I love every last flipping one of them.

"Later," I whisper to Ivy. "We're going to have the best sex of our lives."

"Holding you to that," she whispers back.

I reach for her hand and slide the ring off her right ring finger.

And then, my eyes never leaving hers, I sink to one knee. Because she deserves to be treated like a queen.

"Ivy Scofield," I say, "I can't fly. I don't actually own any leather clothing. And I can't win a swordfight worth shit."

"That's okay," she says. "Because I can't fix an engine, and I *hate* overalls. They give me a wedgie."

It takes us a while to stop laughing. I take a deep breath and get serious.

"But I love you with my body, mind, and soul, and if you will let me, I will spend the rest of my life showing you exactly how much I mean that."

"Me, too," she whispers.

"Will you marry me?"

She grins at me. Not the secret smile. The brightest sunny day smile. "It's very nice of you to ask again," she says, tugging me up to my feet. "But I meant it the first time when I said yes."

From the other side of the door, I hear an avalanche of applause and cheers.

EPILOGUE
QUINN

Miraculously, the Tobuary wedding—to which everyone who helped save the wedding is invited—goes off without a hitch.

No one comes forward to claim that they're pregnant with Tobias's baby or that they've cheated with January.

No one jumps in when the rector says, "Should anyone present know of any reason that this couple should not be joined in holy matrimony, speak now or forever hold your peace."

The invited photographers show up, and the uninvited paparazzi are kept at bay by January's private security.

And Shane and I get to dance together at the wedding that should have, or maybe shouldn't have, been ours. It doesn't really matter because we're so ridiculously happy.

After Shane told me his ring was on my finger to stay, I reannounced our engagement to the Hott siblings and Sonya's friends. Shane and I stopped by Nia and Akemi's place after we left Hanna's so we could reannounce to them, too.

Nia jumped up and down. "You're going to marry Shane fucking Hott!"

"I guess I am!" I said happily.

Then I called my mother in Spain, woke her up, and told her. She had somehow managed not to catch a single whiff of our fake engagement, so she was very excited, in a brand new way, for the real one.

She said we needed to come visit her so she could meet him. Nia grabbed the phone from me and said if she wanted to meet Shane, she should watch the *Crown of Spires* movies. I grabbed the phone back and said she should meet actual Shane because Mavryx was nothing like actual Shane.

"Except for the sword," Shane murmured against my other ear.

Couldn't argue with that.

Now I float in his arms to song after song. His breath sifting through my hair makes every nerve ending in my body stand on end. We've had sex so many times in the past couple of days, you'd think we'd be over it, but I just want him more.

And apparently he feels the same way because he says, "Do you think anyone would notice if we cut out early?"

"No."

We drift, still dancing, toward the door, and then we slip right out the door. If anyone notices, they're too polite to say anything.

Many months later

The Tobuary wedding isn't the last wedding in this story.

Shane and I have two weddings. Of course we do.

We have one wedding for us and another one for the rest of the world.

I'll tell you about the public one first.

Our fans scream for a crossover wedding...so we give them one, on a sound stage in Hollywood custom designed for that purpose. Everyone who's anyone is there—January, Tobias, Brad, George, Leo, Will, Jennifer, Julia, Emma.

Anthony Fessa, however, is absent. When he called me to ask if his invitation had gotten lost, I was in the middle of having sex with Shane, and somehow I forgot to call him back. My bad.

At the wedding, Shane is Mavryx—except this time, his costume and makeup are done by the pros. And holy shit. If I thought the makeshift Mavryx was hot, the professional version has a deeply hydrating effect on my something-blue panties.

Pretty sure he digs the professionally made-up Oriana just as much, judging by the shell-shocked expression on his face when I walk down the aisle in my custom-made mostly white wedding dress, which also features panels of fabric from Oriana's original denim-and-smocking costume.

It's a lot of fun. A really great party. I get to dance with Leo, which is a hoot, and Tom gives me advice about how to make a marriage last.

There are some amazing photos and videos from that wedding. Some of them even go viral—like the one where

Mavryx backs me up against the replica engine and growls into the well-placed mic that as soon as he gets me alone, he's going to carry me off to the end of the universe and keep me there till he's done with me.

Then, even more importantly, there's our *real* wedding...

Everyone *who matters* is there. Shane's sister and brothers and aunt. Easton and his brothers and their wives and girlfriends. Sonya and her posse. Nia and Akemi, our theater students, Nan from Rush Creek Bakery, and, best of all, my mom and her husband (fresh off a plane from Tarragona, Spain!).

When we send out invitations, I ask Shane if he wants me to send one to his dad.

At first he says no. Then, after a particularly wrenching therapy session (yep, he's been going), he changes his mind. He hasn't spoken to his father since his father suggested Shane should get a different manager...but he decides to give it a shot anyway. He sends him an invitation and an email. The email says that Shane wants to give his dad one more chance to show up for him. To be a dad, not a manager. It says it would mean a lot to him if his dad would, for once, support him in something that has nothing to do with acting.

The *yes* RSVP comes back in record time, shocking both of us.

I'm really proud of Shane for speaking his truth and asking for what he wants, and when I look out over the pews in the barn and see Shane's dad sitting there, I get a little teary. Not as teary as I get a few minutes later—but hang on, getting to that.

I mean, we're not expecting Shane's father to win a Dad

of the Year award anytime soon. But maybe he's not a complete loss, either.

Even Weggers is there. He begged Hanna for an invitation. I didn't think she was going to cave, but he was so contrite about misjudging Shane's and my love and so adamant that their granddad would have wanted him there that no one could quite bring themselves to flat out refuse him.

All the flowers at our real wedding come from my garden. The Better Than Sex with Anyone Except Shane Cake comes from Nan's bakery. Kane Wilder does the photography. And Shane's assistant does the videography —because why mess with success?

I wear all white. The top and bottom halves of my dress come from the two dresses we found at the thrift store, and Sonya did an absolutely amazing job of stitching them together—you can't tell they weren't one garment from the very beginning.

("See?" Reggie crows. "There's no reason to buy new.")

Shane wears a tux. When I step through the back door of the Hott Springs wedding barn and we see each other for the first time since late afternoon the night before, my breath catches in my chest. Tears spring to my eyes. Because there he is, so unbelievably beautiful in that crisp shirt and bow tie and sharp black jacket. My guy. Not Mavryx. Not even Shane Fucking Hott. Just the man who's my partner in crime and my best friend, the one who can make me laugh and make me come really hard and then make me laugh again.

And it isn't just new love and infatuation by this point. We've done a lot to prove it will work between us. I've flown down to LA, and he's flown up to Rush Creek. We've traveled together when he's on location, and we've Zoomed and FaceTimed when we can't make any of those things work. And every single minute that passes, I like him more. Admire him more. Want more to spend the rest of my life at his side.

After Shane puts a solid-gold band on my finger and the minister pronounces us married, after Shane kisses the bride (and I kiss right back—maybe a little too enthusiastically if the laughter from the guests is any indication), we get on with the partying.

We eat so much food. We dance our asses off. We hug and chat with and love up all our favorite people.

And then we get in the limo and ride to the airport for our flight to Nepal. To Hotel Everest View.

It turns out that if you want to take your honeymoon at the highest point in the mountaintops and more or less at the edge of the universe, that's your best bet.

You definitely won't hear me complaining.

You might hear me screaming Shane's name a few times, though.

Even Before All the Weddings...

But let's back up just a second. Because even before our dual wedding planning can get into full swing, something else happens that deserves a mention.

The text that touches it all off comes from who else but Arthur Weggers a few weeks after Tobuary's wedding, and it says, *Be in my office at 9 a.m. tomorrow for the reading of Preston's letter.*

After a fitful night's sleep (and lots of speculation about what's in store for Preston), Shane and I are late to the meeting. We were doing okay until he suggested we shower together "for efficiency."

Yeah. No.

Unless *languid*, *steamy*, or *thorough* are the new synonyms for efficient, nope.

We get ourselves to Weggers's office at 9:05. I'm expecting a lecture on promptness, but it turns out we're not the only ones who are late. Quinn and Sonya arrive three minutes after us, sheepish, muttering excuses about breakfast taking a long time to cook. Something about a Maillard reaction gone wrong.

From the high flush on Sonya's cheeks, I'm betting on a totally different brand of chemistry...

"Where's Rhys?" Sonya asks, looking around. "Wait, and where's Pres?"

We've all, of course, noticed the New York brothers' absences...but since other people were still trickling in, no one commented on it.

"They'll be here," Weggers says confidently.

But as the moments tick by, we all start to shift nervously in our seats. Beside me, Shane is growing downright twitchy, checking his phone, his watch, his phone, his watch. Hanna has sent four or five texts to the group chat, and every time—even though I've watched her key in the notes—I jump when my phone buzzes.

"What happens if he doesn't show up?" she asks, biting her lip.

"I can't read the letter unless he's here," Weggers says.

"Okay..." Hanna says slowly. "But what if it says something like, you have twenty-four hours to, I don't know, wrap every building on the Hott Springs Eternal site in Valentine's Day wrapping paper—"

"That would be very frivolous," Weggers says primly.

"Right," Quinn growls. "And Grandfather would *never* do something frivolous to torment us."

"Let's not deal in hypotheticals," Weggers says. "Of course Preston will comply with my instructions—"

Simultaneously, all our phones buzz.

A work thing came up, Preston has texted. *Rhys and I won't be able to make it.*

I look around the room at all the confused faces. Weggers's might be the most confused of all.

Oh. This is going to be interesting.

ACKNOWLEDGMENTS

Thank you to all my readers, who have made it such a fun and joyful experience to bring the Wilders and Hotts to life.

As always, I am deeply indebted to my early readers, Dylann Crush, Christina Hovland, Claire Marti, Brenda St John Brown, Rachel Grant, Sylvie Stewart, Liz Alden, Michelle McCraw, and Elise Kennedy.

Huge thanks also to the author friends who support me on a regular basis—those I've already mentioned, as well as the authors in RAM Rom Com, ECRW, my various Discord servers, and many, many more, including but not limited to Christine D'Abo, Gwen Hernandez, Audrey Nelson, Jessica Auerbach, and Cheryl Cain.

Thank you to my agent, Emily Sylvan Kim, and my sub rights agent, Tina Shen.

Thank you, Mandi Andrejka of Inky Pen Editing. It has been a joy working with you and getting to know you.

Thank you, XPresso Book Tours, especially Giselle, for the release blitz.

Hugs and kisses for my not-author friends who support my imaginary worlds with so much love and patience: Aimee, Darya, Ellen, Elizabeth, Lauren, Molly, Soomie, and Tracey.

To BellGirl, BellBoy, and Mr. Bell, thank you for loving me and letting me love you, which turns out to be the best and most fulfilling thing I've ever done.

Any errors of fact or insensitivity relating to representation are mine and mine alone. If you note any, please let me know so I can fix them, apologize, and learn to be better.

ALSO BY SERENA BELL

Wilder Adventures

Make Me Wilder

Walk on the Wilder Side

Wilder With You

A Little Wilder

Wilder at Last

Hott Springs Eternal

Hott Shot

Hott Take

Some Like It Hott

Under One Roof

Do Over

Head Over Heels

Sleepover

Returning Home

Hold On Tight

Can't Hold Back

To Have and to Hold

Holding Out

Tierney Bay

So Close

So True

So Good (2022)

So Right (2023)

New York Glitz

Still So Hot!

Hot & Bothered

Standalone

Turn Up the Heat

ABOUT THE AUTHOR

USA Today bestselling author Serena Bell writes contemporary romance with heat, heart, and humor. A former journalist, Serena has always believed that everyone has an amazing story to tell if you listen carefully, and you can often find her scribbling in her tiny garret office, mainlining chocolate and bringing to life the tales in her head.

Serena's books have earned many honors, including a RITA finalist spot, an RT Reviewers' Choice Award, Apple Books Best Book of the Month, and Amazon Best Book of the Year for Romance.

When not writing, Serena loves to spend time with her college-sweetheart husband and two hilarious kiddos—all of whom are incredibly tolerant not just of Serena's imaginary friends but also of how often she changes her hobbies and how passionately she embraces the new ones. These days, it's stand-up paddle boarding, board-gaming, meditation, and long walks with good friends.